YOUR FRENCH KISSES

A BOYFRIEND MATERIAL NOVELLA

LAUREN BLAKELY

LITTLE DOG PRESS

ALSO BY LAUREN BLAKELY

Big Rock Series

Big Rock

Mister O

Well Hung

Full Package

Joy Ride

Hard Wood

The Gift Series

The Engagement Gift

The Virgin Gift

The Decadent Gift

The Heartbreakers Series

Once Upon a Real Good Time

Once Upon a Sure Thing

Once Upon a Wild Fling

Boyfriend Material

Asking For a Friend

Sex and Other Shiny Objects

One Night Stand-In

Your French Kisses

Lucky In Love Series

Best Laid Plans

The Feel Good Factor

Nobody Does It Better

Unzipped

Always Satisfied Series

Satisfaction Guaranteed

Instant Gratification

Overnight Service

Never Have I Ever

Special Delivery

The Sexy Suit Series

Lucky Suit

Birthday Suit

From Paris With Love

Wanderlust

Part-Time Lover

One Love Series

The Sexy One

The Only One

The Hot One

The Knocked Up Plan

Come As You Are

Sports Romance

Most Valuable Playboy

Most Likely to Score

Standalones

Stud Finder

The V Card

The Real Deal

Unbreak My Heart

The Break-Up Album

21 Stolen Kisses

Out of Bounds

The Caught Up in Love Series

The Pretending Plot (previously called *Pretending He's Mine*)

The Dating Proposal

The Second Chance Plan (previously called *Caught Up In Us*)

The Private Rehearsal (previously called *Playing With Her Heart*)

Stars In Their Eyes Duet

My Charming Rival

My Sexy Rival

The No Regrets Series

The Thrill of It

The Start of Us

Every Second With You

The Seductive Nights Series

First Night (Julia and Clay, prequel novella)

Night After Night (Julia and Clay, book one)

After This Night (Julia and Clay, book two)

One More Night (Julia and Clay, book three)

A Wildly Seductive Night (Julia and Clay novella, book 3.5)

The Joy Delivered Duet

Nights With Him (A standalone novel about Michelle and Jack)

Forbidden Nights (A standalone novel about Nate and Casey)

The Sinful Nights Series

Sweet Sinful Nights

Sinful Desire

Sinful Longing

Sinful Love

The Fighting Fire Series

Burn For Me (Smith and Jamie)

Melt for Him (Megan and Becker)

Consumed By You (Travis and Cara)

The Jewel Series

A two-book sexy contemporary romance series

The Sapphire Affair

The Sapphire Heist

ABOUT

To do list for my last day of my Paris vacation...

1. Walk along the river

2. Visit all the chocolate shops in the city

3. Wander along the cobblestoned streets.

Things I don't expect to happen...
   1. Meet a charming Englishman while strolling along the Seine

2. Spend the afternoon with him exploring Paris, and kissing. So many French kisses...

3. Board a plane that night wishing I'd gotten his last name.

Besides, you can't fall for someone in one day, especially when you live a world apart...

YOUR FRENCH KISSES

ABOUT

A Boyfriend Material short story
By Lauren Blakely

Want to be the first to learn of sales, new releases, preorders and special freebies? Sign up for my VIP mailing list here!

1

REID

New York

You know that saying about kids in candy shops?

They've got nothing on a fella in a lingerie shop.

Forget lollipops and chocolate bars. I'll take teddies and corsets. Not for me though.

For ...

Who do I want it for?

Who am I kidding? I know how to finish that sentence.

I've known it for three years.

But what are the chances I'll see her again? I've nearly given up. I've been searching, stupidly searching this city for a woman I met once upon a time.

I wander into shops, look in windows, imagining I might see her again.

Someday I'll shuck off that wish for good.

But today?

Today, I still have a smidgeon of hope. After all, I can

recall with crystal clarity the way she curled a hand over my shoulder, showed me a display of pink and white lace, and said it was her favorite.

I sigh, wishing I'd done something different that day.

One thing different.

Regret is an awful taste.

To counter it, I've given myself three months to entertain a quest.

To pop into shops.

Jewelry stores. Clothing boutiques. Lingerie shops.

What are the chances I'll see my five-hours-in-Paris woman?

I don't let myself answer that question.

Because the three months are nearly over.

But today I'm still looking. Today, I still have a chance, one offered to me by the store owner who I met thirty minutes ago.

Peyton extends a hand, gesturing to the shop she's lured me into.

"And this is my little slice of New York. Welcome to You Look Pretty Today," she says. I made her acquaintance in a coffee shop with my good friend Lucas, and she encouraged me to stop in here, luring me with promises of a single woman who likes water parks.

What can I say?

I'm easy. I like water parks.

But does the woman I met in Paris like them?

I have no idea.

See, I don't even know her last name.

Another regret.

This woman can't possibly be the one I've been looking for. But my time is running out, so why not turn over this stone? You never know.

I walk inside and gesture to the shelves of underthings. "I see you have some wonderful items for my nan," I joke.

"I can definitely find something for her," Peyton says. "I have customers of all ages. But right now, I want you to meet my store manager." She guides me through a display of bustiers.

"Got a little matchmaker in you?"

Her eyes twinkle. "I might. She says she has a thing for British accents."

"Lucky for me."

"Yes, it's totally her weakness."

For a dangerous second, my heart beats faster.

But I tell it to settle down.

It won't be her.

Instead, I scan the lingerie on the shelves, my mind ever so helpfully assembling an image of a svelte blonde in one. A lithe brunette. A pretty redhead.

Nameless women. Faceless women. Never her.

As I wander past a shelf of satin shorts, the scent of lavender drifts into my nose, reminding me of gardens in Paris.

Another memory best forgotten.

After today, I will banish all of them and kick this pointless quest to the curb.

I snap my gaze away from the pretty items, my eyes returning to Peyton, who has her hand on the arm of her store manager.

I can't see the other woman's face.

But then she rounds the corner as Peyton says to her, "I have someone I want you to meet."

The store manager steps forward, and I am swept back in time.

Brown hair, brown eyes, a smile for days, and

dimples. *Those dimples.* I swear I'm seeing things. Seeing her.

Someone I never thought I'd see again.

Someone I've desperately wanted to see again.

And I made a promise that if I ever did, I'd do everything different.

Her eyes lock with mine, and I see that day flash across her irises too.

"It's you?" I ask. Then it's no longer a question. It's a statement. "It's really you."

2
———

MARLEY

Paris

Nearly three years ago

I'm not afraid of many things.

Spicy food? Bring it on.

Horror movies? I can handle them.

Camping, hiking, biking, and pitching a tent? Not a problem.

But heights?

Who invented heights?

Clearly someone who hates me.

Heights are officially the worst.

When my girlfriends declare at Café Roussillon over eggs, potatoes, and croissants that today is *the* day, I shake my head. "Au revoir."

"Marley," Bethany says, with a squeeze of my arm and a peppy grin, "You can do it."

She's Rosie the Riveter, tough and badass, but I'm undeterred.

Heights and I don't get along. "I know I can. I don't want to," I say to my college roomie, who wants nothing more than to shoot up to the top of the Eiffel Tower.

"Are you truly saying you don't want to view all of Paris, drink in the vistas, see the Seine cutting across the city like a ribbon?" Emery asks with a sweep of her arm.

I laugh at the image she paints. "You sound like a travel brochure."

"And travel brochures should be followed," she declares as she takes her last bite of egg.

Bethany sips her café noisette—she's gotten me addicted to them—then says, "Paris is for shedding fears."

"And we did that by ordering escargot the other night," I point out as I set down my fork.

Bethany shrugs. "Fine. That was a little terrifying."

"And seriously, thank you for encouraging me, and you are the best, but I swear I have enjoyed seeing the Eiffel Tower from the ground," I say as we pay the check, then leave some euros on the table for the waiter.

"Merci," I call out as we exit and I walk with my friends to the most famous landmark.

This is our last hurrah trip before the three of us scatter across the United States—Bethany to law school in Texas, Emery to a job in San Francisco, and me to business school, starting next week.

Emery pouts. "They say the line will take about two hours, and then we thought we'd do the Montparnasse Tower too. Knock out all the heights today without you."

I nod approvingly. "I like that idea."

"What will you do?" Emery asks.

"Something on the ground," I say playfully as we walk

past a gorgeous stone building with curling ironwork framing the tall windows.

What will I do?

I will wander.

It's the thing I like most.

Walking.

Seeing.

Looking.

"I'm going to meet some fabulous Frenchman," I muse as we enter Champ de Mars, the park at the base of the tower. "Have a tryst in a secret passage somewhere in the city, tucked off on a quiet cobblestoned street; kiss a handsome stranger as Édith Piaf plays; and then have a glass of wine and tell my secrets to the river."

Bethany gives me the evil eye, then looks at Emery. "And why are we going to the top of the Eiffel Tower? I want to go with her and have a secret tryst with a gorgeous Frenchman."

Emery purses her lips, her eyes twinkling. "Dinner's on us tonight if you do have that rendezvous. Because you will be entertaining your besties with details."

I stare at the tower, as if deeply considering the offer. "Let me get this straight. If I have a secret tryst, I get one, a tryst; two, a free meal; and three, the memory of the tryst? Sounds like I'll win."

Emery narrows her eyes and stomps her foot. "She bamboozled us. I want what she's having."

"Maybe you'll have a secret love affair at the top of the tower," I say, then hug my best friends goodbye, telling them I'll meet them later, since we need to get ready to leave for an insanely early flight.

I stroll along Rue Saint-Dominique, stopping along the way to check out displays in jewelry stores and clothing boutiques, before I pop into a chocolatier.

A red-haired man behind the counter nods, smiles, and says, "Bonjour."

"Bonjour," I reply, then I ogle the displays of mouth-watering sweets, choose a few, and leave with chocolate in hand.

I cross the boulevard and find a bench by the river. "It's just you and me, river," I say to the water.

I grab a truffle and bite into it. As decadent caramel spreads on my tongue, a man I didn't notice at the end of the bench turns and smiles.

"Good morning."

3

REID

My team came in third, but I can't complain because we didn't even think we'd place.

Tenth was more like our goal.

Hell, *not* finishing in last place would have been an achievement for the Road Flyers, my amateur bike team that competed in a four-day race ending in the City of Lights. It surprised the hell out of the four of us when we landed a spot on the podium.

Tour de France contenders we are not, but it was a right adrenaline rush. Now I'm enjoying a few hours in Paris before I catch a flight back to London, my team-mates having taken off already. I'm booked on a different flight.

I pop a chocolate square in my mouth, savoring the orange zest flavor in the dark chocolate, when a brunette with a spray of freckles across her cheeks takes the spot at the end of the bench.

She gazes at the river with a happy sigh, then says, "It's just you and me, river."

My brain is a pinball machine, lighting up, buzzers whirring.

I barely speak a word of French, and she has an American accent. Perhaps it's my lucky day.

"Good morning," I say.

She jerks her gaze to me, then smiles. "Good morning to you too." Her eyes drift to the bag from the shop. "A kindred spirit, I see."

"Well, you know what they say." I gesture to the chocolate like there's some well-known saying about it.

She arches one brow, and it's wildly adorable the way it rises, matching the corner of her lips quirking up. "I don't know what *they* say. What do *they* say?"

I lower my voice, cup my mouth, and stage-whisper, "They say it's never too early to eat chocolate."

"Ah, yes. I have heard that," she says with a nod, dipping her hand into the bag. "I believe it's called chocolate o'clock."

"That's the time my watch is set to as well."

"I have truffles. Want one?" She waggles the bag, and I adopt a new truism immediately. *When a pretty woman offers you chocolate, you say yes.*

"I would love one. As long as you promise they aren't poisoned."

Her expression is intense, overly serious. "As an avid and well-known poisoner, you have my solemn vow," she says, then offers one.

"Well, since it's a solemn vow . . ." I slide closer to her on the bench just as she slides closer to me. I snag a chocolate. "I'm going to trust it's not laced with arsenic."

She scoffs. "Please. I'm all about cyanide. It's stronger and faster."

I stop, chocolate midair. "How do you know that?"

She laughs, a bright, cheery sound. "I read a lot of

mysteries. I can tell you the ten deadliest poisons, and the ones most likely to go undetected. But the look on your face is priceless, like you really thought I was going to off you."

I take the chocolate, pop it in, and bite. "I'm living life on the edge. Taking my chances."

"Go you."

When I finish, I hold up my bag of treats. "Want one of my deadly sweets? I made sure to pick up the botulinum-laced variety," I say in a macabre voice.

Her eyes twinkle. "Best morning ever. This is like Russian roulette with chocolate." She chooses a square, then moans around the chocolate. "Oh, that is divine."

So are your lips.

So are your sounds.

"Glad you like it," I say, as a horn honks. I glance at the river where a boat bleats as it winds its way along the Seine. One of those three-hour cruises perhaps, and something I'd considered for my last day in Paris.

But as much as I enjoy the view of the river and the idea of a day on the water, I like the view on the bench so much more.

And the chance that may be next to me.

I didn't think I'd place in the bike race.

But I went all out.

No reason to do anything differently with the chocolate poisoner. The gorgeous brunette looks to be in her early twenties, only a few years younger than I am. Maybe she's as single as I am too. "I'm Reid. I'm from London. I was in Paris for a bike race with my team. We placed third. I'm heading home tonight."

Her smile is magnetic. "I'm Marley. I'm here with friends before I return to New York to start business school."

I extend a hand and shake hers. "Pleasure to meet you, Marley."

"And you too, Reid," she says, holding my hand longer than I expect as she studies my face. Then she takes a breath, like she's preparing to say something.

And I hope it's not that she needs to leave.

But I don't want to miss a chance to enjoy my last few hours here to the fullest, so I speak first. "There's a new shop a mile away. Fancy a chocolate tour?"

4

MARLEY

It's like he can read my mind. "I was going to ask you the same thing."

One eyebrow quirks. "If I wanted to go on a chocolate tour?"

I wave my hand in the direction of a bookstore I've heard about. "Well, actually to a bookstore. But chocolate works too."

He strokes his chin, like a detective noodling on a case. "Were you going to share all your favorite mysteries featuring death by poisoning?"

I grin mischievously. "I was indeed."

His expression shifts as a delighted grin lights up his handsome face, highlighting his square jaw and his soulful brown eyes. "Chocolate always works, but so do books."

He rises.

I dust off my hands, grab my bag, and tuck the chocolate into my purse. I eye his chocolate bag. "Want me to carry your chocolate?"

He clutches it, pretending to squire it away from me.

"A poisoner and a chocolate thief? I've been warned about your type." He wags a finger at me.

"And yet you're walking along the Seine with me," I tease as we stroll.

"True. Apparently, I am easily enchanted by American accents," he says with a wry smile as we wind past a street lamp, and he hands me his bag of chocolate. I tuck it into my purse.

"Your British one isn't too shabby," I say, and then I dive right into questions. Because I can. Because clearly this is a day that is bursting with possibilities and none of those options require holding back. I can't help but think Bethany and Emery will be so jealous, but I'm not doing this to make them jealous. I'm doing this because it feels like what a last day in Paris should be like—a walk beside a river with a handsome stranger, full of potential and flirtation. "You're from London and heading home tonight?"

He nods as we reach the corner of the street, and I let my eyes roam over him. Jeans and a gray T-shirt. He looks about twenty-four or twenty-five. "My bags are packed, and I'm ready to go," he says, and there's the slightest hint of sadness in his voice.

Funny, I feel a touch of it too already. A touch of missing. That's so odd because I've spent only a few minutes with him.

But already we click.

Instantly. Incredibly.

And that's why *not* spending another hour with him in this city would be a missed opportunity.

"Mine too," I say, choosing to enjoy this time fully.

"Are you headed home today?"

"Tomorrow morning. At the crack of dawn," I say

with a frown. "Why do six a.m. flights even exist? We have to be at Charles de Gaulle at four thirty."

He shakes his head. "They should be abolished. When I'm in charge of all things, I will outlaw flights at ungodly hours."

"Thank you," I say, like I'm imploring his graciousness. "You have my vote for prime minister."

His brown eyes seem to twinkle. "I thank you for your support." He takes a beat as we cross the avenue. "Have you enjoyed your trip so far, Marley? Summer in Paris can be lovely or vicious."

"It's been lovely. We went to Italy and to Spain and to Paris."

"Quite the jaunt."

"I know, and I'm so lucky we were able to pull this off. My friends are at the top of the Eiffel Tower now, but I didn't want to do that. I happen to detest heights."

"You do?"

I nod, like I'm confessing. "They make me nervous. Like, I can see all the ways they can go wrong. I picture flinging myself down from the top story, and well, that kind of ruins them."

"That would definitely do it."

"Are you afraid of anything? Like, anything totally irrational?"

"Just your standard fear of poisoning by chocolate. But that's hardly irrational," he says with a wink. "Tell me more about your trip."

I picture the last few weeks, recalling our adventures in Rome, our meanderings across the city of Barcelona, and our time in Paris these last few days. "We did it on a shoestring budget," I explain. "We'd made a vow to take a European trip when we graduated, especially since we're all heading in different directions. One of my friends is going to law school. The other starts her first job."

"And you're going to business school?"

"Yes. And while I'm there, I hope to figure out what exactly I want to do in business someday."

"Ah, work. Yes, I've heard of that. It's so dreadful when it gets in the way of bike races and chocolate shops. Shall I ask if you've given any thought yet to what you want to do, or is that a topic best avoided?"

I shrug, but it's the happy kind, because it doesn't entirely bother me that I don't know. "Is it crazy to say I'm not sure? I do want to run my own business. But I'm torn. Sometimes I think I might want to work in public relations and open my own firm. And other times I think I want to market new fashion lines. But I also really like just talking to people, so maybe I should open a cute little boutique, and then it'll turn into a whole line of cute little boutiques. Or I could start a coffee and chocolate shop," I say, tossing out that last option.

"Do you like coffee?"

I adopt a serious stare. "Like it's a religion."

"I pray at that altar too. So, I say you should open a café that sells clothes and then do your own PR for it."

I snap my fingers like I have all the answers now. "There you go. Now I know what I want to do."

"See? It was serendipity that we met," he says playfully as we weave past a Frenchwoman pushing a trolley full of groceries, a baguette poking out the top of one bag.

"But I'll miss Paris," I say, glancing at the bread, then at this man by my side who doesn't feel like a stranger at all. Nor does he feel like the handsome guy I just happened to bump into. He feels like a guy whose path I was meant to cross.

We slow our pace at a light. "I'll miss Paris too," he says as he holds my gaze longer than I expect.

I should look away. I should break the moment. But I don't. Because my stomach flips. And tingles spread down my arms. Then I whisper, "I'm glad I'm afraid of heights."

The light changes, and we cross.

He glances at me out of the corner of his eye, then smiles. His smile is fantastic. So warm and inviting. "I'm glad you're afraid of heights too."

5

REID

I wouldn't say we gorge ourselves on chocolate, but we come damn close.

Marley is a fiend when it comes to sweets, with a sweet tooth that matches mine. I tell her as much as we regard the carnage of our chocolate fiesta on the table—those little wrapper things that hold the chocolates are completely empty. "We have officially made this morning chocolate o'clock every damn second."

"We have," she says, straightening her shoulders like she's issuing a declaration. "And I regret nothing."

"I regret nothing either."

She sets her chin in her hand and meets my eyes. "So, Reid. What do you do in London when you aren't devouring chocolate?"

I lean back in the chair, diving into the quick details. "I'm a designer. I studied graphic design at university. I'm working my way up now, but someday I'd like to have my own company."

She smiles. "I love that. Love that you know what you want to do. What is that like—to know?"

I ponder her question for a few seconds, maybe more. "It's like . . . normal. If that makes sense? I think I've always known. I've loved drawing and designing, and it was always my path. I like this path. I'm glad I'm on it."

"What can you draw?" There's a curious glint in her eyes.

"I happen to be a fantastic doodler. But I'm also tops at drawing caricatures of American girls in chocolate shops."

A laugh seems to burst from her. "Are you serious?"

"As serious as a heart attack." I head to the counter, ask the shopkeeper for a pen and napkin, and return to her, doing a quick rudimentary sketch of her face. It's great fun, because it gives me free rein to stare at her the whole time, to study the shape of her cheekbones, her big brown eyes, the freckles dotting the bridge of her nose.

She sports a grin the entire time, like she's delighting in this moment. I certainly am—it's an unexpected morning in this city with her, and I don't want it to end.

When I'm finished, I show her the napkin.

She chuckles. "That's adorable."

I preen in an over-the-top fashion. "I am known in many parts of the world as an adorable doodler." Then a spate of nerves crawls up my spine. Do I ask her if she wants to keep this? Is that too much for whatever this brief encounter is? This random date that's careening toward its inevitable end in hours?

She speaks first. "I'd like to keep it. May I?"

My chest warms. "It's all yours, Marley."

Neither one of us says anything for a moment. We simply look at each other. Sparks race over my skin, across my chest. This thing, this chemistry, it can't go anywhere. But right now, it feels like we're somewhere special.

And I don't want today to end until it must. I only have a few hours, but I want to spend them with her. "Do you believe in happiness?" I ask.

She tilts her head. "Of course. Why wouldn't I?"

"Do you believe it's possible though? Is it worth chasing?"

"Often I think it's the only thing worth chasing," she says, then adds with a sigh, "but sometimes responsibilities get in the way."

"They do. So you seize your chances for happiness."

"Are you happy?"

I smile. "I'm pretty sure the way I feel right now is the very definition of the word."

The look on her face is magical, like I've said the one perfect thing, so I do my best to keep up my winning streak. "Do you want to go to a bookstore?"

I'm rewarded with another smile. "I would love to. That's the other definition of happiness."

6

MARLEY

The bookstore is quiet, and the delicious smell of pages drifts through the shelves. Patrons lounge in well-worn leather chairs, reading books of poetry or tales of love gone awry.

Truth be told, I have no idea what they're reading, but it feels like that's what they must be inhaling. Or maybe they're devouring stories of strangers who meet for a moment in time, who connect in an instant electric burst, then the firecracker fizzles out, leaving the night pitch-black.

For a second, a storm cloud descends on me.

That's what today is with Reid. I knew that when we first rose from the bench and wandered along the river.

We're a moment in time. A starburst. A spark against the sky that burns bright and fast.

But I'm embracing it.

Even though there's a part of me that's wishing, wanting for today to last beyond this date on the calendar.

Only that's silly.

Today is what it is.

A day.

Heck, it's a few hours. A moment in time.

And time should be cherished.

We walk past a table that holds gift books, including a coffee table one with photos of Paris. I run my thumb across the cover then open it, flipping through the images. I point to the ones I like best. Paris in the rain. Paris in the snow. Paris in the sun. "This makes me happy too. These pictures."

He flips to an image of a café. "And that does the trick for me."

I set down the book, and we wander through the mysteries, whispering about poisons and butlers and deadly nights. The steps creak as we head up the staircase to the second floor. It all feels so European. On the second floor, we wander through the stacks of English-language titles.

He picks up a book with a sad-looking man on the cover, staring forlornly into the distance. "He's having a bad day, isn't he?" Reid whispers.

"A terrible one, but if you get that book, yours will become worse."

"I'll return it straight away," he says, tucking it back on the shelf, then stepping closer to me. "Perhaps I should find a book that will only make the day better." He takes a beat. "But that would seem impossible."

I look down, then at him, and smile. My stomach flips when he holds my gaze. "I agree." I lick my lips, then continue along the aisle, where I grab a book with an image of a skillet on the front. *"Top Skillet Recipes to Change Your Life."* I tap it. "This will make your day amazing."

He nods seriously. "That's true. That does look like a day-brightening book."

"It's your typical airplane read," I tease as we walk past an alcove with an old typewriter perched on a tiny oval table. A handwritten note on the typewriter's keys says *Drink each day.*

I stare at it for a long time. Reid does the same. "Is that a directive to grab a pint?"

"I don't think so," I say pensively.

He gives me an inquisitive look. "What do you think it means, Marley?"

"I think it means drink each day down like it's delicious."

His brow furrows like he's considering this. "That's what you take away from it?"

"I do," I say, feeling certain. "Drink, savor, indulge."

His brown eyes darken as I say those words. "Those are some delicious verbs."

"See? That's what I mean. When you read it that way, it changes the meaning. It's not the best recipes for skillets that will change your life. It's *savoring*. Like the day is a glass of your favorite wine," I say, lifting an imaginary glass. "And you enjoy every last sip."

He's quiet as he seems to study my face, then he sets a hand on my back as we make our way to an open window, stopping to stare at the cobblestoned streets below.

I'm keenly aware that he hasn't removed his hand from my back. Just the slightest touch without being too much, too presumptuous.

But I wouldn't mind a little presumption.

"Do you enjoy your days like that? Like the note urges?" he asks.

"It's hard to say. I've just finished college, and that's not entirely the place where you can or should drink each day. But I think that's why I've enjoyed this trip so much. I've tried to set aside all the unknowns of what will happen in business school. What I'll decide to do. I'm trying to just enjoy every moment, then learn what I love so I can decide what type of business I do want to run someday. What about you? Do you savor the days?" I ask.

"I don't know if I always do. Sometimes I worry too much about work. The future. What I'm going to do next. The next step. The next job."

"I worry about that too. But I try to tell myself there will be time for that."

"I should take a page from your book and do that too," he says, bumping my shoulder. "Like what I did there?"

I groan, smiling though, because I like contact with him. "I like it a lot."

As he stares out the window, his gaze seems to land on a lanky Frenchman trundling by on a bike. The cyclist holds a bouquet of red balloons.

I laugh, tickled by the image. "He's enjoying his day."

"He's drinking it down." Reid takes his hand from me, and I instantly miss it, wanting it back.

But instead, he reaches for my hand, threading his fingers through mine. His touch lights me up like sparklers on New Year's Eve. "That's better."

Tingles spread across my body. "Are you drinking the day?"

He smiles, and it's both naughty and happy. "This is a day I want to enjoy every last drop of."

"Me too."

We head downstairs, and he grabs a book. The photos

of Paris. He buys it, then gives it to me. "This makes me happy. Keep it."

I know I will keep it always. Someday when I'm seventy, I'll look at it and remember the afternoon I spent in Paris with the man from London who made my heart beat faster and harder than it had before.

The clock is ticking.

That can't be avoided, but I can't let it dictate my every thought.

This is exactly what it is.

A dessert, a drink, a treat.

You don't get to have chocolate for every meal. But you damn well better delight in it when you do.

With her hand in mine, we cross the bridge over the river, passing tourists snapping selfies. We could take a picture. We could exchange numbers. Share the image. But then what?

Trade little texts while she's in New York going to school and I'm an ocean away?

Instead, I squeeze her hand and I focus on the here and now. Only that. Taking mental snapshots. Making memories I can call up. Something I do little of in my digital life. But I want to live fully in this incredible, real moment. "This is the most perfect day. I just want you to know that."

She smiles at me, and it makes my heart flip.

That's unexpected.

Frankly, a little inconvenient too.

Because that'll make it harder to get on the plane. And I have to get on the plane.

"I know that," she says in a bit of a whisper.

"And do you know what would make it even better?" I ask, continuing down this carpe diem path because it's all I can do here.

"Is there anything that could truly make it better?" she asks, a little tease in her tone.

The sound of her voice, a little naughty, a little flirty, winds through me. "Well, there *are* a few things."

Her eyes dance with dirty thoughts. "I can think of a few things too."

"More than a few," I add.

"Lots. So many things."

I groan. "You're going to make this day quite hard. But truth be told, I was thinking we should walk around the Luxembourg Gardens."

She lifts her chin, licks her lips, and says, "Take me there."

How can a woman sound innocent and naughty at the same time? But she does. She absolutely does, and I love it madly.

* * *

We wander through all sorts of flowers. I don't know the names. Or the kinds. Maybe they are irises or lilies. Possibly tulips.

Marley seems to know them all, as we walk through rows of flowers, bursting with color, ruby red and bright pink and sun-drenched yellow.

She rattles off the names, but not like we're in botany

class. More like "I've always loved irises" or "Tulips are nature's flirts."

"Are you a tulip?" I ask.

She spins around, wiggles her eyebrows. "What do you think?"

It's a loaded question, and I'm pretty sure I know the answer.

I step closer, inches away. The air is charged, buzzing with possibilities. Somewhere beyond the walls of the garden, the city rolls by.

But here, the garden is an escape with a woman I didn't know mere hours ago. A woman I will say goodbye to in another few hours.

A woman who has lips that look so damn kissable.

"Right now," I say, holding her gaze, "I'm not thinking."

I lift my hand and stroke a thumb along her jaw. She gasps, then whispers, "Don't think."

"I'm definitely not thinking one bit," I say as I move closer, my lips so tantalizingly near hers.

"I'm *only* feeling," she whispers.

I thread my fingers in her hair, press my lips to hers, and drink in a kiss.

I savor every last drop.

I indulge.

And I memorize.

Because I don't want to forget this kiss.

This day. This moment.

It feels different from other moments.

She's different from other women.

Soon we'll go our separate ways, but I always want to remember the American woman I met one afternoon in Paris before I had to catch a flight.

That's how I kiss her.

Like I'll never forget the taste of her sweet lips, the softness of her breath, the way she melts into me.

Or maybe I melt into her. Because this kiss goes to my head. My mind is a blur, and my body is humming sweet yet dirty music as I kiss her softly, tenderly.

Then a little bit harder.

She feels so right in my arms that I have to wonder if I believe in love at first sight.

But that's rubbish.

That's not the way of the world.

That's not the way of *my* world.

Only, for a few stolen moments, it feels like it could be.

Like with a handful of afternoons that spill into the next and the next, we could become that.

She slinks her arms around my neck, bringing me closer, her body pressed to mine.

Yes, a few more days of this, and I'd be in love with her for the rest of my life.

That's the problem.

8

MARLEY

I'm not going to claim to be an expert on kissing.

Sure, I've had my fair share of locking lips. But it's not as if I keep a list of kisses, and if I did, the ratings would be "good, but not great."

When Reid kisses me, I know this is great.

I know this is some kind of kiss.

His lips are soft and confident. His touch is both tender and electric. And he smells so damn good. Like soap and pine and man. My senses are throwing a party as this stranger in a strange land lights me up with his lips, his touch, and something else too.

Something intangible. Something wonderful.

Something that I know will be over far too soon.

Is that why this kiss is so incredible?

Because it exists in its own parallel universe, one where I'm staying in Paris, and he's living here, and we're spending the evenings together wandering the passages and cobblestoned streets as rain falls? Of course, it'll rain in Paris in our universe as we kiss at cafés and shops and under street lamps.

And we make plans to meet again tomorrow.

That's what this kiss is.

A kiss for tomorrow.

A kiss that is tinged with wistfulness, with longing, and with a wish for it to be more than one kiss.

A wish for it to last.

But it can't. Because we're both leaving.

I break the kiss, and he looks lust-drunk.

It's so sexy, and I want to put that look on his face again and again.

"Wow," I say.

"Yeah," he says, scrubbing a hand across his jaw.

"That was . . ."

"Incredible?"

I give him a flirty grin, shaking my head. "Nope."

His brow creases. "No? Am I going to need to try harder?"

"I won't object to that, but I was simply going to say I'm pretty sure it was the best kiss in the history of first kisses."

He leans in close again, dusting those lips over my cheek to my ear, then whispering, "I want to keep writing in that history book."

This man.

This man and his funny, clever, vulnerable ways.

"I want that too," I say, but because we can't have what we want, he takes my hand and we walk through the gardens toward the exit.

"I hope I'm not being presumptuous, but I'd like to spend the rest of the day with you until I leave."

I lean my shoulder against his. "You can presume away."

As we exit the gardens, he says, "So, Marley. What would you do if you lived here in Paris?"

"Like, for a job?" I ask as we turn onto a block teeming with pretty boutiques.

"Actually, I wanted to know what you'd do with me, but sure, we can start with work."

"Reid," I say, laughing. "Don't be silly."

"Why is that silly?"

I tap my chest. "I'd do you," I say, bold and direct.

He stops in his tracks, blinking, then drags a hand through his hair. His gaze turns hot, and he reaches for me once more, bringing me close. "You are magnificent."

"So are you."

Then he shows me what a second kiss for the record books is. My knees go weak, my skin sizzles, and I record this moment too.

But, like all of today has so far, it ends too soon. We resume our pace. "So, to answer your question, I'd probably do something where I could talk to people. Maybe work in a shop."

"I'd come to your shop every day."

"Stalker much?" I tease.

He scoffs. "Please. You'd be mine if we lived here. I'd come to your shop at the end of the day, and we'd walk to a brasserie, sit down, order a glass of wine, and watch the city go by. All while we were in our own world."

I swoon, my heart shimmying for him. "Are you the most romantic man I've ever met?"

His grin is so delicious. "I better be."

I run my fingers down his shirt. "You are. It's official."

We walk past a stationery shop selling pens and gorgeous writing paper. The thought briefly occurs to me that we could keep in touch, send letters, little notes.

But keeping in touch seems far too dangerous.

Like leaving out a tempting treat you couldn't actually have.

"Anyway, so what would we do after dinner?" I ask playfully as we pass a jewelry store peddling lockets.

"I'd find all the most romantic places in the city to kiss you again. Since you need to fill in a whole history book of entries."

"So I would record those kisses?"

He nods exaggeratedly. "I would fully expect you to. Record, tabulate, rate."

"You want me to rate your kisses? Maybe I already am."

He tugs me into a quiet alley framed by an arch and curling ivy, and seals his mouth to mine, dropping a hot, tempting kiss on my lips before giving me a hot, naughty stare.

"Are you trying to set a record?" I ask, my skin heating up.

"What would the record be exactly? What's the category?"

"The category is winding me up."

"And I trust it's working?" he asks, a devilish quirk on his lips.

"Everything you do is working."

He smiles, but it fades into a sigh as he presses his forehead to mine. "I wish . . ."

A lump rises in my throat. "I wish too."

"I wish I had another night here. I wish my plane wasn't leaving this evening."

"I wish we could slow down time."

"I wish I met you yesterday." He stops. "Is that crazy?"

I shake my head. "No. But I'm glad I met you today. And I'll miss you tonight."

He swallows, exhales. "It would be crazy, right?"

We both know what the other isn't saying, but I say it anyway. "To see each other again?"

"Yes, I want to. But how can we?"

I shake my head. "I don't know how we could without upending everything."

"I know." He sounds as sad as I feel. "I want to see you again, Marley. You have to know if things were different, I'd take you out tonight, and tomorrow, and the next day. I wouldn't think twice about calling you. Or texting you. I wouldn't take days. Or hours. I'd ask you now and I'd see you tomorrow."

My heart thumps harder for him. "I'd say yes, Reid. I'd definitely say yes."

He presses a kiss to my forehead. "But I live in London."

"And I live in New York."

"And we just met," he adds.

"And I don't know what I'm doing with my life when I finish school."

"You might wind up in Alaska."

I laugh, shaking my head. "Doubtful, but you never know. I do have to focus though. Use the opportunity to figure out what I want to do. I have a scholarship. To keep qualifying for it, I need to hit a minimum GPA. That has to be my priority."

"As it should be."

I draw a deep breath, prepping myself to say something hard. "We need to just enjoy this for what it is."

He smiles, one corner of his lips curving up. "One perfect afternoon in Paris?"

"The most perfect one ever recorded."

"Let's keep making it better," he says, and that seems like a fair enough deal to me.

9

REID

There is no doubt.

I can't imagine looking back on my life and ever having had a better day.

In fact, it's so damn good that I'm tempted, more than I've been tempted before, to do something wildly ridiculous.

Like try to stay in touch.

As we walk by the Tuileries, I want to say, *Screw this long-distance issue. Give me your number and let's talk.*

But what would that look like? Late-night phone chats? All-day-long texts that would distract me as I tried to work my way up at the firm and as she went to school?

That's mad.

So we talk now instead. I ask her about her favorite things.

She tells me about her friends, how Bethany is a hugger and Emery is a giggler, and how the three of them were like sisters in school, depending on each other, helping each other through painful breakups and even more painful exams.

When it's my turn, I tell her about my sister and how we've always been close friends. I talk about the books I love, the articles that capture my interest, and my allergy to early mornings. I also confess that pop music is brilliant.

"Pop like Taylor Swift or Katy Perry?" she asks.

"Or P!nk or Lady Gaga."

"Whoa. I like you." She squeezes my arm.

"Thank you. I was hoping I'd pass the pop music test. And that you'd have the same taste in music."

She arches a dubious brow. "Did I say I had the same taste? I'm a Bruce Springsteen gal. Bryan Adams. And the Eagles."

"What generation are you, woman? Lost in time?"

"I like Jackson Browne too."

"Are you secretly fifty? Were you born in the seventies?"

"I'm retro."

"You can call it that, but I've never met anyone with a seventies retro kink."

She wiggles her brows. "Maybe that's not my only kink."

I groan. "That's a door I'm going to kick wide open. What are the others? I require details. Each chapter, and every sordid verse," I say as we pass a boutique with a pink window display showing off teddies and bras, panties and stockings.

"I have a wicked fetish for lingerie," she says, pointing at all the lacy numbers.

"You do?" I ask, my voice gravelly, thick with a new bout of lust.

She stares longingly at a white-and-pink bra with

some sort of crisscross straps. "That's my favorite. I never bought a lot of lingerie in college since it's expensive, but I have always loved the prettiest things. I love looking and touching, and I love the way wearing them makes me feel."

I loop an arm around her waist. "How does it make you feel?"

She turns to me and whispers, "Beautiful."

My body longs for her. My mind aches for her. I bring her closer, unable to resist kissing this woman. "You are beautiful," I say, as I kiss her one more time.

A slow and lingering kiss.

If I'm not careful, I'll ditch my flight simply to spend one more night with her.

The thought is tempting. So damn tempting.

And once it lands in my head, the idea that I could do that? It's too powerful to ignore. "I could stay another night," I blurt out.

Her eyes flutter open. "Tonight?"

"Yes. I know it sounds crazy. Insane, even."

"No, it doesn't," she says. "But . . ."

I swallow roughly. "But what?"

"But what if I don't want to get on my plane in the morning?"

"Then you'd stay here with me," I say, even though we both know that's a foolish dream. I won't be here either.

She ropes her arms around my neck. "Fine. I'll stay here with you, and we'll dance on a rooftop garden, and we'll watch the stars. We'll go to The Marais and duck in and out of antique shops, and pop into the Musée Rodin whenever the mood strikes."

I pick up the thread easily. "There are Monets to be seen. Don't forget the Musée d'Orsay."

"We'll kiss in front of a Van Gogh that's rumored to

be magical. And then there will be more magic when we go clubbing in Oberkampf."

I groan appreciatively. "I like your story of our romance. Clubbing in Oberkampf sounds dirty and delicious."

"That's how we'll dance, Reid. Our bodies will be tangled together."

"Inseparable," I add, my voice going low, smoky.

"People will watch us," she says. "They'll pretend not to, but they won't be able to take their eyes off us."

"They'll be jealous of the young lovers," I add, stroking her hair, running a thumb across her jaw, picturing our sultry nights.

"They'll be jealous because they'll know that when we leave, we'll be *that* couple."

"The couple who can't take their hands off each other."

"Or their eyes," she adds.

I can't stand this. I can't take the tension. Or the reality that I'm leaving and so is she. I press a kiss to her lips, then ask the inevitable. "What would happen if we stayed in touch?"

She looks up at me, and her voice comes out trembling. "What do *you* think would happen?"

The look in her eyes. The tremor in her voice. I have to stop pushing and pressing. She's going to graduate school. She has no room for a long-distance lover.

But this stupid organ in my chest is galloping out of control. I try to talk back to it. *For fuck's sake, it's been four hours.*

But what if four hours is enough?

Enough to know?

Enough to feel?

Enough to try to stay in touch with a woman going to business school halfway around the world?

Exactly.

I must focus on goals. Hers, and mine. She doesn't need a man distracting her from her studies and scholarships with nightly texts. And I don't have the wherewithal or the means to travel to New York to see her regularly.

I dig down deep, then answer with my brain. "We'd fall for each other and it would mess up our lives. That's why we're going to do something else."

Her brow knits. "What would that be?"

I grab her hand, lead her into a café, order two espressos, and ask her for the book from the store. The Paris photo one.

"You're taking it back," she says with a pout, clutching it.

"I would never do such a horrid thing. I have other plans for it."

She proffers it from her bag and slides it across the table to me.

I ask for a pen, and she hands me that too.

I write inside.

Someday when I run into you again, because I know I will, we'll have more than one perfect afternoon. We'll have endless time.

I turn it around and show her.

Her expression shifts. A lone tear streaks down one cheek, then another.

But she seems to collect herself, because she straightens her shoulders and says ever so softly, "I believe in that someday."

I look at my watch.

He looks at his.

There is no more time.

But I want to squeeze every last second out of this fantastic afternoon. I walk with him to his hotel, where he hands the porter a few euros and the man brings him his bag from bell check.

Reid turns to me. We stand in the tiny lobby with music playing softly in a romantic language. I can't make out a word, but I know it's a sad song, a story of lovers torn apart.

"Come here," he whispers.

"I'm already here."

"I want to give you my last name. I want to know yours too. But if I do, I worry I'll spend all my time googling you."

"I know that's all I'd do, so we probably shouldn't." I swallow down the stone in my throat. "This is crazy. How is this possible?"

With a smile, he shrugs, then says wistfully, "French

kisses?"

I smile back, full of melancholy too. "Your French kisses."

"Our French kisses." He cups the back of my head, then lowers his voice. "You have to know I want to say screw responsibilities. I want to say I'll see you tomorrow. But I'm not going to say that."

I shake my head, my throat tight. "You can't say that. I can't either."

"And you shouldn't. But today is making me believe in something else."

My heart speeds up. "What's that?"

"That if we both believe in happiness, we'll find it. We'll remember this day fondly. And if it's meant to be, we'll find each other again."

I love the thought, but how can that happen? "How? If I try to find you, I won't be able to do the things I need to do."

"Don't try now. Go to grad school. Somehow we'll meet again." He whispers in my ear, "And when I see you again, I won't get on a plane. I'll take you home with me."

I bury my face in the crook of his neck, wondering how I went from being afraid of heights to being afraid of falling in an entirely different way.

I let another tear fall, then I pull back, fasten on a smile, and tell him the full truth. "And when you ask, I'll say yes."

We leave the hotel. He hails a taxi, and it's here far too soon.

Everything is ending far too soon.

But somewhere deep inside, I keep hoping it's only the beginning.

Especially when he gives me one last kiss.

Then we say goodbye.

11

REID

London

A month later

I don't think about Marley.

I don't let my mind wander to the lovely American woman with the freckles.

I refuse to let my thoughts stray to her soulful eyes, her lush hair, her winning smile.

And I do not under any circumstances consider her warm sense of humor, her wryness, the way she teased me coupled with the ways she didn't tease me. My God, the woman was so open, so heartfelt.

I'll never meet someone like her again.

But I don't think about that whatsoever.

If I did, I'd be a sad sack.

And I'm not. At all.

I have work to do, a business to build, and contacts to develop.

And that's why when I go to New York for a project, I don't look her up.

How could I?

I don't know her last name.

Sure, I could search all the Marleys in New York in business school. But there are many business schools in New York, and surely many Marleys. So if I did that, I'd have to punish myself with no more football, no more books, no more chocolate.

I'd have to ask my best mates to take away my man card.

She was a moment in time.

And only that.

And as I once read on the back of a book jacket I designed, "Some relationships were meant to last for a lifetime. Some for a day."

My chest punches.

What a stupid saying.

I should have asked for her name, her number.

I should have done any or all of the above.

Except I won't and I can't.

After a meeting, I walk through the Village, past the NYU business school.

Is that where she went?

No idea.

But just in case, I give myself an hour.

One hour to sit.

To think.

To hope.

It's insane in many ways.

Not to mention completely pathetic.

But I can't seem to stop.

I don't want to stop.

I want to see her. And walk up to her and say, *Let's do that over.*

But when sixty minutes pass and there is no Marley, of course I resign myself to the cold realization that what happened in Paris was meant to be one perfect afternoon.

Nothing more.

And over the next two years as I travel back and forth to New York and make contacts and network with American designers on shared projects, including a fella named Lucas, I force myself to move on from Marley.

I even date.

It's horrid, but so it goes.

12

MARLEY

New York

Two years later

I survive.

I survive two years of business school.

I make it through the toughest classes of my life.

And I survive missing the man I spent the most magical afternoon with.

For a while, I didn't think I would.

I was certain I'd break down, fly to London, and knock on all the doors of all the design firms.

But I didn't.

We made an agreement.

That we'd rely on fate.

That serendipity would have to bring us back together.

So I didn't look for him, and while I wasn't searching, I found something else in two years of classwork.

Myself.

My goals.

My dreams.

And I might even know what I want to do.

Someday I want a shop that becomes one of many. I plan to open a boutique that women flock to and love, and then I'll open more.

But first I need to start with a basic J-O-B.

I'm offered jobs at banks and accounting firms.

But I turn them down.

Because I can't stop thinking about something I said in Paris.

I'd probably do something where I could talk to people. Maybe work in a shop.

I'm still drawn to that.

When I'm offered an entry-level job at a lingerie shop with the potential to move up, I jump on it.

It might not sound like a sexy offer for a business school grad, but it works for me. It's a chance to learn the ropes.

And I'm determined to find my way.

I do that every day for the next year, figuring out how to run a business, understanding what it entails, and helping customers every day.

A woman named Olivia comes to the shop once a month or more, and we chat about travel, life, and lingerie.

"My fiancée has a thing for lingerie," she tells me in a whisper on one of her visits. "But then, so do I."

"Sounds perfect that you both love it," I say, then I show her some of our new styles, and she oohs and ahhs.

As I ring her up, we chat more, and she asks me if I plan on going back to Paris anytime. I sigh, a little wistfully. "I hope so. I'd love too. I spent the most wonderful day there."

She studies my face for a few seconds. "Did you fall for someone in Paris once upon a time?"

I startle, surprised. Am I that easy to read? Maybe I am. "Something like that."

"Then I hope you find your something like that again," she says, and as she turns to leave, she offers a smile and says, "Maybe you'll find him again."

"Maybe I will," I say but I'm not sure I believe that.

So I focus on other matters.

The store, my skills, my work.

I become friendly with my boss, even more so when she falls in love with her best friend, and it's reminiscent of how I felt in Paris. Fine, she's known this guy for ten years and I knew Reid for five hours, but those five hours marked me.

They marked my heart, and I kept them close.

The memories are as sharp as they've ever been.

I'm not a nun. I haven't held out for him, because that would make me foolish. But I haven't met anyone who makes my heart trip like that man did.

Which feels infinitely silly when I let myself break it down like it's a business problem. It seems like math ought to defy the probability of that happening.

But nothing about that day seemed like math.

And it has stayed with me.

Maybe it always will.

* * *

One day as I'm helping Peyton plan the next season's looks, a British man walks into the store. He's older, in his fifties, and he's charming as he buys a nightie for his wife.

"Thank you two lovely ladies so very much," he says when he leaves.

I sigh. "I love British accents," I admit to Peyton.

"You do?"

"I do. I met this guy once in Paris for a day. He was British, and ever since then, I swear I perk up when I hear an Englishman. Like I'm hoping it might be him."

She smiles. "Maybe someday it will be."

I shake my head. "That won't happen."

"You never know . . ." she says, letting her voice trail off. "Where is he?"

"I don't know. I don't even know his last name. I only know where he lives and his profession."

"You could try googling him."

I have tried. I've punched in every permutation of "Reid" and "London" and "design firm." But I've found nothing. I wish I had one more detail. One more clue. Something else to add to the search string. Something that would lead me to him.

But there are none.

That night when I'm home alone, I open the book and read his inscription.

Someday when I run into you again, because I know I will, we'll have more than one perfect afternoon. We'll have endless time.

I trace the words.

Then I close the book and send a thank you to the universe that I had that moment.

That's all it'll ever be.

I look at the napkin drawing one more time, hoping I'll find his name. His number. A secret message. But I've turned it over a thousand times, and it's only a drawing.

And a memory of a moment, a small slice of time.

The most wonderful moment I've ever had.

One I miss terribly.

* * *

In the morning I wake up with a start, a tingling sensation in the back of my mind. Déjà vu. Like when you see an actor and can't place him until you remember he was the third guy on the left in episode seventeen.

It's there.

One more detail.

I was in Paris for a bike race with my team. We placed third.

Reid said that to me.

Will it be enough?

I swallow nervously, grab my computer, and send a wish out to fate.

Anticipation builds in me as I google "bike races in Paris" during the time I was there.

And I find one.

My heart speeds up. It races like a locomotive along the tracks as I scan the names of the teams, then the members.

And I gasp.

Because there it is.

Reid Martin.

My whole body is tense, alive with possibilities.

I drop the name into google, and I gasp in a whole new way.

He's a designer.
And he lives in New York.

I spend the morning trying to figure out what I'll say when I email him at work. But I don't plan what to say if he walks into the shop that afternoon.

I am speechless.

13

REID

I check out a florist on the Upper East Side.

I pop into a jewelry store in Murray Hill.

I stop by a lingerie shop in the Village.

It's getting to be a habit with me.

But it's one I can't break.

I haven't broken it since Lucas asked me to set up shop with him in New York a few months ago. We'd already been working together on a number of projects, and most of our clients were in the city. It only made sense to pack up my bags and follow the business.

That's what I'd been building toward for the last few years in London.

I didn't move here to find her.

I moved here for business.

Yet looking for her has become a hobby.

Perhaps I am a stalker.

Or maybe I'm just a guy who can't quite give up.

I give myself a deadline.

I tell myself that I'll allow myself three months of checking out shops, of looking for her in person, since

I've had no luck finding her through online searches. I simply don't have enough details.

Instead, I check out places she might work.

I'm like a detective chasing down clues.

But I'm reaching the end of the line.

Until the day some of my business partner's old friends show up at a coffee shop and tell me I must come along to a lingerie store.

What are the chances it'll be hers?

But it's my last chance, so I take it.

And then I see the face I've been dreaming of.

14

MARLEY

I'm seeing things.

There is no other explanation.

There is no other reason.

I can't possibly be looking at Reid.

Reid Martin, who I've been composing an email to in my head all morning.

He looks just as handsome as he did that day, if not more so.

"It's you," he says in a whisper laced with disbelief.

"It's you," I say, trembling, unsure too.

Because when your wildest dreams come true, you still don't believe them.

After all, he could be married. He could be involved. He could have thought we were foolish.

"How are you?" he asks, the most pedestrian of questions, as he walks over to me, wonder in his eyes.

"I'm great," I say in a voice that hardly feels like my own. It's like I'm talking from within a dream. "And you?"

"I've never been better. Literally."

"You look . . ." My voice trails off. It's choked with emotion. I don't want to let on that I've dreamed of this magical moment. But I can't fake it.

"You look real. You look like all I've wanted," he says, taking the leap first.

It unlocks my heart. It unlocks everything I've stored up since I met him and we spent the most magical day together. "I missed you."

"And I made a promise in Paris."

"What was that?" I ask, my voice pitching up.

"That if I found you again, I'd make sure we spent a lot more than five hours together."

I beam. Like the sun is shining inside me. I look at my watch. "What do you know? I have no place to be and nothing but time."

His smile matches mine as he takes my hands. "Have dinner with me tonight. And tomorrow. And the next day."

15

REID

That night

That part about feeling like a kid in a sweet shop?

That's nothing compared to a man waiting for a date with the woman he can't get out of his head.

I never believed in *the one who got away* till I met her.

Till I *let* her get away.

I had my reasons at the time.

They made sense in my head.

And I knew, too, in my heart that we weren't a possibility. There was too much between us then.

Now?

I'm determined to make sure the woman I've been searching for doesn't slip through my fingers.

As I wait at the restaurant, I adjust my tie, then smooth my hands down the front of my trousers. I grab my whiskey and knock back a thirsty gulp, then I look at the time again.

Time.

The thing that mocked me three years ago.

Now, my life is different.

The question is . . . will hers be?

The door opens.

I turn around. My heart skips all its beats.

She walks in, looking as innocent and as seductive as she did three years ago along the River Seine.

Those freckles.

Her eyes.

Her curves.

And what's that?

A hint of a pink bra strap.

I groan.

She walks over to me. "Good evening."

I say nothing.

I made a promise to myself that if I had the good fortune to see her again, I'd do something else first.

Something that made me lose my mind for her.

I stand, sweep a hand through her hair, and tug her close for a kiss.

It's like going back in time.

It's as fantastic as I remembered.

She's soft and warm, and she kisses back with a hunger I didn't forget. I didn't inflate. I didn't exaggerate.

This woman kisses me like we're kismet.

Like we're serendipity.

Like we simply met at the wrong moment in time, but fate was on our side, guiding us back to the right moment.

Because now is right.

When we break the kiss, she smiles like she has a naughty secret. "It's a fact— best first kiss ever."

"Was that our first?" I ask with a grin that I can't erase.

"It's the first of many more to come," she declares.

This woman.

I'm not letting her go.

I take her hand, guide her to the table I reserved, then tell her, "Just so you know, I'm not letting you get away this time."

She squeezes back. "Just so you know, I'm not going anywhere."

"I have one question though," I say.

"Go for it."

"Do you like water parks?"

"I love them."

"Excellent."

We have dinner and we catch up, and it's as magical as it was that day nearly three years ago.

But more so.

Because it's not winding up.

It's unfurling into the future.

That's where I go with her that night when she invites me to her place. Well, I go other places too. I take her to the heavens and back, and she calls out my name countless times, and I say hers too as she digs her nails into my back.

But it's all the future.

She's my future.

In the morning we exchange numbers, and I send her the first text from beside her in bed.

Reid: Just so you know, I'm falling in love with you.

Marley: Just so you know, I've been falling in love with you for three years.

The time is finally right. It's finally ours. And with a little bit of searching, and a whole lot of fate, we have what I wrote in the book that day in Paris.

Endless time.

THE END

Want to be the first to learn of sales, new releases, preorders and special freebies? Sign up for my VIP mailing list here!

If you haven't read the other titles in the sexy, romantic comedy series BOYFRIEND MATERIAL, you're missing out! Be sure to start with ASKING FOR A FRIEND, a fun, flirty office romance you'll love! Available everywhere!

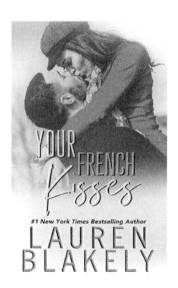

TOO GOOD TO BE TRUE

ABOUT

To say I'm wary of love would be an epic understatement. Keep that four-letter word far away from me.

But then a matchmaker friend insists she can pair me with the perfect man for me.

Even when sparks fly and chemistry crackles from the first date, I refuse to believe this kind of insta-connection can be the real thing.

Even though for the first time it feels like it could be.

Or is it just too good to be true?

1

Olivia

Do I want to try it?

My brother asked me that very question when he invited me to check out a prototype for his new home automation system.

This is no Alexa. This is no Google Home. His home automation system supposedly answers your most annoying emails, makes you an omelet, and even folds your laundry.

Well, in my dream life it does.

Geek that I am, naturally I said "hell to the yes" when he invited me to take a test run. So here I am, race-walking across the blond hardwood floor of the lobby of his swank Gramercy Park building and pushing the button to his penthouse apartment.

When I reach the top floor, I practically vault down the hall to his place.

Can you say eager?

I bang on his door. He takes more than ten seconds to answer, so I decide to act thoroughly annoyed when he finally does.

"Come on, come on, come on." I'm bouncing on my toes, making grabby hands.

He rolls his eyes from behind his black glasses. "Overeager much?"

He holds the door open for me. I sweep in, my eyes like lasers scanning for the little white device. "You can't dangle something as cool as the ultimate home automation in front of me and expect me not to jump all over it and want to play with it. I only strapped a jetpack on and flew down to touch it."

He laughs, escorting me to the living room. He knows that, just like him, I love all sorts of electronics, gadgets, gizmos, and toys, and have ever since we were kids, fighting over all sorts of various game consoles. Since I'm the oldest, with two twin brothers, I usually beat them.

And I beat them up.

Someone had to put the little evil geniuses in their place. Lately, it's hard to put Dylan in his place since he's been traveling for business. But when he returns, I fully intend to kick his butt in our softball league.

"True, true," Flynn says thoughtfully. "What was I thinking? You and Dylan are both geeks like me."

I hold up a fist for knocking. "Dude, we are so nerdy. Also, FYI: nerds rule."

He scoffs authoritatively. "You know it. Nerd or bust."

I spy the device on the coffee table. My eyes widen and I hold out my hands, like I'm caught in a tractor beam. "Take me to your leader."

"Kate is all yours," he says, using the name of the automation device.

I park myself in the leather couch and fire off questions.

"Kate, tell me a dog joke."

"Kate, make me a sandwich."

"Kate, what's the weather like in Bora Bora?"

She answers each one with panache.

What's more amazing than a talking dog? A spelling bee.

Okay, you're a sandwich.

And . . .

Perfect, you should go there.

I glance at Flynn, who's rightfully proud of his new tech. "Kate knows the answers to everything. I'm booking a flight now."

Flynn nods his agreement. "Bora Bora is always a good idea. If anyone thinks otherwise, you should excise him or her from your life."

I tap my temple. "The Bora Bora litmus test. I'm filing that away." I return my focus to the white disc. "Kate, make me a playlist of top pop songs."

As she preps some Ariana Grande and Katy Perry, Flynn groans and drops his head into his hand.

"No, please, no pop songs."

"I like pop."

"You need to try indie rock, I've told you."

I roll my eyes and launch into my best rendition of his favorite tunes. "Oh, my life is so sad, I flew with an eagle, and now I have a noose around my toes."

He cracks up and gives me the strangest look. "What on earth is that, Olivia?"

I answer like it's obvious. "That's what indie sounds like. A sad lament."

"Oh, well then, let me tell you what pop sounds like." Flynn adopts an intensely happy look, snapping his fingers, then sings a send-up of my music. "Oh, I want you. Yes I do. Yes, yes, yes, I do. Do do do do do do do do do."

I laugh. "See, that's so fun to listen to! You should totally write that song."

"So we agree to disagree on music."

"But not the Bora Bora litmus test."

"Never the Bora Bora litmus test."

I spend the next hour playing with the device, and pronounce it is the coolest one I've ever seen. "But we have one more test for Kate."

"What is it?"

I hold my arms out wide, like I'm ready to make a pronouncement. "This will be the toughest test of all. Can she handle what I'm going to throw at her?"

Flynn gestures grandly. "Go for it."

I clear my throat, adopting a most serious tone. "Kate, find me a hot, smart, and kind guy. Must love animals. Be willing to try quirky new dates in New York City. Ideally, likes odd and interesting art installations. And be able to sustain a conversation about something other than himself."

Flynn's eyes bulge. "She's not a miracle worker," he says protectively. He's protective of the device.

Kate speaks back in her calming robotic voice, but I've rattled her. "I'm sorry, that does not compute. Can you please try again?"

I crack up.

"You can't really expect her to do the impossible," Flynn says.

"I know, tell me about it."

He leans forward, hands on his knees. "So is dating getting you down?"

I sigh. "A little bit. It's kind of awful out there. Have you tried it lately?"

He shudders. "No, I'm practically on a sabbatical since Annie."

I shudder too, remembering Flynn's ex. She turned out to be completely using him, trying to sink her claws into his fortune. Not for nothing, but it's really hard for a tech multimillionaire to find somebody who likes him for him. My brother is rich as sin, and normally I don't feel bad for him, but on this count—never knowing if someone loves you for you or your money—my heart is heavy.

It's a poor little rich boy dilemma, as he calls it. Yet it's wholly real.

"But what about you? What's the latest from the minefield of dating?"

"Last night I went out with a handsome surgeon, who was all around pretty funny and smart. But it turns out he's into jazz music," I say, crinkling my nose. "He spent half the time telling me he loves to go to jazz clubs *and* to listen to jazz at home. I had to be honest—jazz is never going to be part of my life, so we're clearly not compatible. We'd never see each other."

Flynn gives me a look, takes a deep breath. "Olivia. But are you doing it again?"

"Doing what?" I ask, indignant. "Being direct and honest on dates about what works and doesn't work?"

"Are you sabotaging every date you go on?"

I sit up straight. "I do not do that."

He points at me. "Yes, you do."

"I don't care for jazz."

"I'm sure you could have found a work-around for his love of jazz. Instead, you sabotage. You've done that ever since Ron."

I huff. "Do you blame me? Ron was the ultimate douchenozzle. And he hid it well."

"'Douchenozzle' is a bit tame for that specimen. More like 'king of all the assholes ever.' It's not often you find a man who's not only a cheater but a serial cheater. He had affairs like it was an advent calendar."

A twinge of embarrassment stings my chest. "And that makes me the stupidest woman ever for missing the signs?"

Flynn moves next to me, squeezing my shoulder. "No. You liked the guy, and he was the Artful Dodger. It was hard to spot his deception at first. But ever since then, when you've met a guy here or there who seems somewhat decent, you always find something wrong with him. A smart and funny surgeon? But he likes jazz, so that's a deal-breaker? And then you tell him?"

"But I don't like jazz one bit," I say in a small voice.

"Look, I don't like jazz either. But I don't think it needs to be a line in the sand." He arches a brow. "Be honest with me. Are you constantly looking for what's wrong with a man so you won't get hurt again?"

I sigh, wishing it wasn't so obvious, but then Flynn knows me as well as anyone. "I was totally hoodwinked by Ron. I didn't see it coming, and I should have. What if it happens again?" I ask, my deepest worry coloring my tone.

"Anything can happen, but now you try to find something wrong with someone before you even start. You're never going to open yourself to what you want if you do that."

I cross my arms, exhale heavily. "Fine, maybe I do that, but look, I haven't met anybody that ticks all the boxes on my checklist. Or even three quarters. Hell, I'd settle for half. I don't even know if my dream guy exists."

He stares out the window, like he's considering a math problem. Since my brother solves math problems in his sleep, he snaps his fingers. "My buddy Patrick. His sister is a matchmaker."

"A real matchmaker? Like Yente?" I sing a few lines from *Fiddler on the Roof*.

"Of course, you have to sing that every time you see her. It's literally required. Why don't you try Evie? Let her know what you're looking for. Maybe she can find someone for you."

I've tried online dating. I've been set up by friends. I've been open to meeting men at the gym, at bookstores, even at the farmers market. But I've had no luck finding a jazz hater, animal lover, quirky-art fan, who's hot as hell and likes me.

"Admittedly, I'm kind of picky. Do you think I'm better off being single?"

"Olivia, you want to be happy. You want to find someone. Just call Evie. Her job is to find matches for picky people."

That sounds exactly like me.

And because I'm not boneheaded, I do call her. I meet with her the next day at a coffee shop.

She's everything you want in a matchmaker. She has a keen eye for people; she's perky, wildly outgoing, fantastically upbeat; and she knows everyone.

"Are my requirements just too crazy?" I ask after I've told her what I'm looking for.

Evie gives me a reassuring look and pats my hand. "No. You don't have requirements that are too hard to meet. What's too hard is to find a man like that online. But that's why you came to me." Her smile is radiant and full of confidence. "I have a few men in mind. Just give me a couple of days, and I promise I will do everything I can to find you the man of your dreams."

It sounds impossible to me.

2

_____

Herb

"Hey there, little Cletus. You're doing great, and you look swell," I tell the teacup chihuahua with the burnished brown coat. He whimpers as I stroke a hand down his soft back. Cletus is resting in a cage after the five-month-old had a very important surgery today. "Don't worry," I whisper. "You won't miss them."

My vet tech snickers behind me. "Bet he will."

I roll my eyes at David as I turn around. "I see you're suffering from neutering sympathy. Shall I get him a pair of neuticles to make you feel better?"

"That would help me a lot, come to think of it."

"You do know he doesn't miss them?"

David grabs his crotch. "I'd miss mine."

"Then it's a good thing I'm not neutering you, isn't it?"

At twenty-three, David is still young, and his age might be why he still feels that associative pain that men often experience when a dog is neutered. At age thirty-four, and after thousands of spays and neuters, I'm well beyond that. I don't get emotional over removing that particular part of a dog's anatomy. And I don't get weirded out.

It's all in a day's work.

David gives me a salute. "Yes, boss. Also, Cletus's foster mom is here."

"Great. I'll go chat with Evie." She's a regular foster for one of the city's nearby rescues, bringing in little dogs for their nip and tucks as they're getting ready to be adopted.

Gently, I scoop up the pup and carry the coneheaded boy to the lobby of my practice on the Upper East Side.

Evie waves brightly at me. "And how is the sweet little boy?"

"He did great."

Evie laughs. "Now, I always thought it was kind of funny to say that an animal did great during a surgery. Because, really, isn't it *you* who did great during a surgery?" She taps my shoulder affectionately.

She has a point.

And I concede to it, blowing on my fingernails for effect. "When you've got it, you've got it. No one snips dog balls better than this guy."

"Put that on your business card, Herb."

"It'll be my new tagline." I shift gears. "All right, you know the drill. Give him plenty of rest, make sure he takes it easy. He might not want to eat right away. And whatever you do, keep that lampshade on him."

Evie drops her face into the dog's tiny cone and gives him a kiss. "I won't let you get out of your cone, I prom-ise, Coney Boy."

"Give me a call if anything comes up, okay? Day or

night. Doesn't matter."

"That sounds perfect." But before she turns to leave, she gives me a look. It's a look that says she has something on her mind. "Dr. Smith, I've been meaning to ask you something."

"I can see the wheels turning in your head."

She smiles, acknowledging that I'm right. "Have you started dating again? It's been more than a year or so since Sandy left."

"Yes, I've dated," I say, a little defensively. "I just haven't met the right person."

"It's hard to meet the right person. I hear you on that front." Her tone is sympathetic.

"I thought I *had* met the right person."

The thing is Sandy was a fantastic woman, and I can't fault her for leaving. She was offered a fantastic job in Beijing. She accepted and boarded a flight two weeks later without any fanfare or discussions about us continuing.

We'd been together for a year. We'd started making plans. And then her plan was to move halfway around the world, so that's what she did, ending us in one clean slice.

"But you can't let it get you down," Evie adds. "You are a prize."

I straighten my shoulders and flash an over-the-top smile. "Thank you. I always thought I'd look really nice paraded around onstage, perhaps given away at the end of a blue ribbon ceremony."

"We'll enter you in a dating contest." She sighs thoughtfully, her eyes narrowing a bit as she taps her chin with her free hand. "But I have other ideas for you."

"Fess up. Are you trying to enlist me into your stable again?"

She swats my arm affectionately. "Of course. I've only been trying to get you in my stable for ages. You know that. Smart, single, sweet as anything, clever, hot vet who does free spay and neuter clinics for the city's rescues? You are going to be in demand."

Since she's a premiere matchmaker, Evie's broached the subject before. I've been reluctant though. Maybe I've been nursing my wounds since my ex took off with barely a goodbye kiss. Or maybe a part of me figures if I can put myself through vet school, open a successful practice, and make it in Manhattan, I ought to be able to find a woman without a little assistance. "Honestly, I figured I'd meet someone the old-fashioned way, like how I met Sandy. We bumped into each other at a coffee shop. She nearly spilled her hot chocolate on me."

"Ah, the old rom-com meet-cute."

"Well, yeah. I suppose it was. So I assumed I'd meet someone new in a similar fashion."

"And how's that working out for you?"

I scratch my jaw, considering her question. "Badly."

"You don't say?"

"Do I detect a note of mockery?"

"No. I simply agree that it's as hard as differential calculus to hope to meet someone in person in a random, swoony, just-like-the-movies way."

"I've been on dates. Mostly setups from friends."

"And?"

I wince, shaking my head. "Dreadful. I'd rather bathe in molasses than go out with another *oh, Tonya knows so-and-so and so-and-so knows so-and-so*. And what it truly amounts to is this—your one single friend was pressured by his girlfriend or fiancée to set up her one single friend, and it doesn't matter if you have anything in common."

She nods sympathetically as she strokes Cletus's head. "That is indeed the problem with friends setting up friends simply by virtue of their relationship status. I, however, have a long list of lovely single ladies, and I only connect people I think—no, I'm sure—will go together like gin and tonic."

"I do like a good gin and tonic."

She smiles impishly. "I know. All my clients are vetted and interested in the real deal. And I know you're interested in that too."

"How do you know?" I'm curious why she says that, but truth be told, she nailed it on the head.

"That's what you wanted with Sandy. You're not somebody who goes out and plays the field, Herb."

She's right on that count. "That's true."

She stares at me, determination etched in her blue eyes. "So, what's it going to be, Mister Meow?"

I groan. "No. That nickname is unacceptable."

"I promise I won't call you that again if you'll let me match you."

"So it's coercion now, eh?" The woman is relentless with her cheer and optimism.

"Call it coercion, or call it kismet. Whatever you call it, I have the perfect woman for you."

I raise a skeptical brow. "What if she's boring?"

She shakes her head. "Not a chance."

I toss out another concern. "What if she's shallow?"

"She's bright and thoughtful."

And one more hurdle. "What if she, I dunno, smells?"

Evie leans in closer and taps my nose with her finger. "She smells pretty, you silly man."

Then the deal-breaker. "What if she doesn't like dogs?"

"Give me some credit. As if I'd set you up with

someone who doesn't like dogs. The woman I have in mind is lovely. She's been looking to adopt just the right three-legged dog."

And my heart melts a little bit. Wait, wait. I can't. I can't fall for her that quickly, I don't even know her. "I suppose one date can't hurt. But I don't want to do dinner."

"Dinner is off the table."

"I don't want to do a wine tasting."

"Just say no to the vino."

"I don't want to do a beer tasting, and I don't want to do something that's like super hipster-y, like a mayonnaise tasting or pickle tasting."

"Got it. You probably don't want to do a carrot tasting either, then. Do you?"

"Do people really have carrot tastings?"

"Have you been to Brooklyn? They have everything these days."

"True that."

"You want to do something totally unconventional. Something that will let you know if you have chemistry."

That's the thing. I've done the whole typical three dates thing a handful of times ever since Sandy left, and I don't want to get on that merry-go-round again. "I just want to get on the merry-go-round once for one date, and I'll know after one date."

"Then it needs to be one spectacular date. Do you still like bizarre, oddball, quirky modern art?"

"Damn, you have a good memory."

"I have a memory for matches. Would you like to meet a smart, sarcastic, tech-savvy art lover who likes to discover all the interesting things about New York and who loves puzzles?"

My ears perk up. "I love puzzles."

3

_____

Olivia

"How do I look?" I ask my brother on the other side of the phone via video chat.

His green eyes light up with laughter and, admittedly, a whole ton of mockery. "How do you look?" he echoes.

I bristle. "I need a guy's opinion."

"And you asked me?" He points to his chest.

"I'm pretty sure you're a guy. Is there something you want to tell me? Did you swap your parts?"

"No, but my point is, I'm your brother. It basically disqualifies me from ever commenting on your appearance."

I huff. "Can you just tell me if I look good?"

"No, I actually can't tell you. I couldn't function any longer as a man in any way if I tell my sister she looks good. Fine, empirically, yes. You look good. But you also look stupid because you're my sister, and I have to think that."

"You legitimately cannot think your sister looks nice in something? I'm thirty, you're twenty-seven. We're not children anymore."

"Doesn't matter. Certain things can never change. You look fine. Sisters always look fine. I can't give you any other opinion than that."

I stare daggers at him. "Flynn, it's a good thing I like you. And you know what? I like myself too, so I am going to assume that I chose wisely in the fashion department."

He flashes a smile. "There you go. That's the confident sis I know and love. You did choose wisely. Now go out and have a great time. I'm so psyched that you used Evie. I have a good feeling about this. Don't sabotage it."

"Who, me?" I ask ever so innocently. "I would never do that."

His expression goes stern. "I mean it, Liv."

I hold up my free hand in oath. "I promise. I installed an anti-sabotage shield on myself tonight. And I am going into this with eyes wide open."

We say goodbye, and I give myself a final once-over in the mirror.

Jeans look good, boots look sexy, cute top that slips off one shoulder is pretty, with a hint of something more. My brown hair sports a little wave as it curls over my shoulders.

"You are a thumbs-up," I tell my reflection.

I head downtown to Tribeca to meet Herb, the hot vet.

* * *

I arrive right on time, expecting him to be late. Most people usually are. But when I see a tall, trim, toned, handsome, as in the most handsome in the entire universe, man standing in front of a light installation at the Helen Williams Gallery, my breath catches.

There's no way that's him.

That guy in the dark jeans and a blue button-down shirt that hugs his muscles has to be somebody else. I bet he was flown in, shipped in from some foreign country that grows good-looking men in meadows. He was paid to stand around and simply radiate handsome. He has to be a model. There's no way that's actually Herb, the hot vet, standing under a fuchsia-pink light, exactly where Evie said to look for him.

Herb is probably in the restroom and this stepped-out-of-a-magazine-ad man is holding his spot.

But then Mr. Too Handsome for Words catches my gaze. His lips quirk up in a lopsided smile that puts all the other lopsided smiles in the entire universe to shame. Because that is the crooked smile that defines why crooked smiles are absolutely delicious. Already my stomach is flipping, and I haven't even talked to him.

"What do you think? Is pink my color?" he asks from a few feet away, glancing up at the light.

God, I hope it's him. I walk closer. "I see you as more of a magenta."

He gives me a thoughtful look. "That's too bad. I was actually hoping perhaps I would be a periwinkle."

I laugh. "Do you know what periwinkle looks like?"

"No, isn't it a shade of, let me guess, blue?" He extends a hand. "I'm Herb Smith."

Praise the Lord. "I'm Olivia Parker."

Herb Smith is the most handsome man I've ever met, with his dark hair, square jaw, and blue eyes the sapphire color of perfect Bora Bora ocean. The man is to die for, and I don't believe in playing games. If I'm going to be up-front with the duds, I'll be direct with the un-duds.

"I didn't think the man standing under the light was actually going to be you," I admit, going for full truth.

"Why's that?"

I gulp, and then I bite off a big chunk of honesty, since what's the point in anything else? "You look like you were imported from the land of hot men."

He blinks. His eyes widen and sparkle, and then he says, "Wow. I didn't know that country existed."

"It's right between Goodlookingvia and Stunninglandenero. Just north of Beautifulcountria."

"I'd like to see your map of the world."

"I have it at home. But was that too forward? Calling you good-looking and objectifying you from the start? Want me to rewind and go again?"

"Hold on a second. You just complimented me for being too handsome, and you think that was too forward?"

"In case you think I'm only evaluating you based on your appearance," I say, since I had the impression from Evie that her services are more of the soul mate variety and less of the hop-on-the-hottie style.

He runs a hand lightly down my arm. "Judge me some more. I should be so lucky."

He drops his arm and I smile, the kind that stretches across my whole face. "In fact," he adds, "I hope you have a long list of traits you're going to be evaluating me on, like a checklist?"

I wave a hand dismissively. "I have that list on my smartphone. I'll fill it out tonight. After we see how this goes."

"How long is that list?"

I stare up at the ceiling, pretending I'm deep in thought. "I'd say it's about five or six pages."

"You're a woman after my own heart."

"Do you have a long checklist?"

"I do, and it's incredibly long." He takes a beat, his baby blues strolling up and down my body. "Lots of things are incredibly long."

"Who's forward now?" I ask, acting all aghast, but I'm not aghast at all. I like long things.

"What can I say? It seemed apropos. By the way, I'm not imported. I was actually locally grown."

"Ah, so you're a farm-to-date man?"

"Yes, I was homegrown within a fifty-mile radius. Raised in Westchester. So you're really able to tick a ton of boxes tonight. Presuming farm-to-date is on that *long* checklist."

"I'm adding it now and checking it off," I say, and inside I am punching the sky.

This is the best date ever.

As the pink glow from the neon light installation flickers behind him, I decide to opt for more honesty since it seems to be working so far—and way better than sabotage, it turns out. "I probably shouldn't say this, but dating can seriously suck, and in the first ten minutes, you're more fun than anyone I've gone out with in a long time, and on top of that, you're an insanely handsome guy." I park my hands on my hips, narrowing my eyes. "What's wrong with you?"

He heaves a sigh. "Fine. I'll admit it. I'm terrible at following IKEA directions for putting furniture together. I know, you just follow the steps. But it's hard, and I am bad at it. Can you live with that?"

I frown, scrub a hand across my chin. "If I have to."

He steps closer, his eyes taking a tour again. "Also,

you beat me to it. You're beautiful. But honestly, even if you were average looking, that would be fine too, because looks aren't the most important thing, and these first few minutes are my favorite too. In a long time."

Holy shit. He's a breath of rarified air. I'm smiling, he's grinning, his eyes are sparkling, and my insides are shimmy shimmy bang banging. "I agree. Looks aren't all that."

"So we're good, then? If you bore me, I'm gonna be out of here in like a half hour."

"That long? I'd have thought sooner. But I'm glad that the challenge is on, and it goes both ways. You better keep up with me, Herb Smith."

"Oh, I intend to. I absolutely intend to keep up with you."

We wander around the gallery, checking out the bizarre installations made of neon lights, and as we go, my skin warms, my heart squeezes, and my hope skyrockets. I like this guy, I like his ease of conversation. I like the way he snaps, crackles, and pops when he talks.

I bet there's something wrong with him though.

Except I can't go looking.

I need to maintain the anti-self-sabotage shield.

We stop in front of a bright yellow pair of neon lights that look like a balloon animal at certain angles. "Also, can we get one thing out of the way real quick?" he asks.

I slice a hand in the air. "There's not going to be any sex tonight."

Laughter seems to burst from him. "That's not what I was going to say, but it's good to know your ground rules. Just so we're clear, are all types of sex off the table?"

Twin spots of pink form on my cheeks. "Probably."

He steps closer, and I can smell him—his aftershave is

woodsy and intoxicating. "What about kissing, can we kiss? Let's say that I meet some of the marks on your checklist, do you want to have a kiss at the end?" he asks, and I'm nearly drunk on him already.

I want a kiss right the hell now. "That seems reasonable," I say a little breathy. Then my mind trips back to his comment. "What did you want to get out of the way, then?"

He takes a deep breath. "Yes, Herb is my real name."

"I didn't think it was a fake name."

"Who would pick that as a fake name, unless you were trying to scare somebody off?"

"Your name doesn't scare me," I say, because I'm 100 percent unperturbed by his old-school name.

"Are you sure?"

I point to the light sculpture on the white wall. "I'm still standing here under this weird, bizarre, twisty-turny collage of rainbow neon lights. I'm sure."

He glances up at the art installation in question. "Isn't that the coolest thing?"

"It's so weird, it's like the perfect weird piece of art. I want to hang that in my apartment and have people come over and say, 'What is that?' And I'll reply with 'my innermost thoughts,'" I say, all haughty.

"You're devilish," he says in admiration.

"Perhaps I am."

I stare at him, amazed that it's already going this well. "By the way, why did you mention your name?"

His tone is softer, more direct. "I guess because I'm surprised you didn't. Most dates bring up my name, since it's unusual. They want to know if it's a nickname, if it's real, if it's a family name that my mom *had* to give me. Or a mistake."

"A mistake? Why would someone think it's a mistake?"

He shoots me a steely glare. "Herb? Let's cut to the chase. It ain't Chase. It isn't Hunter or Bennett or Foxface, or whatever cool names dudes have these days."

A smile crosses my lips, warming me from the inside out. "I don't give a foxface if your name is cool or uncool. But is there a story behind it?"

He chuckles in a self-deprecating way that's thoroughly endearing. "Herb was my granddad's name. It was supposed to be my middle name. But he passed away a few days before I was born, and well, my sentimental parents made it my first name."

"Aww. That's touching. A very sweet story."

"I'm stuck with it, but he was a great man, so it's all good. And I have the world's simplest last name, so go figure."

"I like both of your names. The juxtaposition of the old-fashioned next to the familiar is a refreshing combo. It makes you even more unique, like this date."

"Normally on dates I count the seconds until it's going to be over."

"Ouch. The seconds, really? Is it usually that bad that you have to count the actual seconds?"

He nods vigorously. "It's usually that bad."

"What's the shortest date you've ever been on?" I query as we stroll through another hall of the art gallery.

"I would say about twelve minutes and fifty-two seconds. We had nothing to say to each other, and it was evident when she wanted to talk about how to do her nails, then she showed me an Instagram video of how to do nails, and there was like sponges and glue, and it was Instagram. Have I mentioned it was Instagram?"

"I'm going to go out on a limb and admit it. I do not

get the fascination with every single life hack for every single thing, for every type of makeup or every type of possible decoration you could put on your body or face, but it seems like everyone in a certain age range wants to do everything they've learned from Instagram."

He smiles. "Is it too early to say this is the best date I've been on in a long time?"

My grin matches his. "I don't think it's too early at all, but I think we really should reserve judgment until we finish the main attraction."

"Are you ready for it?"

"I'm so ready."

We finish the appetizer portion of our date and head over to devour the main course.

4

Herb

As we walk to the warehouse, we talk.

"Ever been to an escape room before?" We turn down a lively block in Tribeca.

She wiggles her eyebrows. "That sounds like a come-on."

"Maybe it is." I dive into an exaggerated seductive voice. "Want to come see my . . . escape room, baby?"

She purses her lips then drags a hand down her chest. "Oooh, yes. Show it to me now."

I growl, keeping up the routine, loving how easily I'm clicking with this woman. "Level with me. Are you an escape room virgin?"

She drops a demure expression on her face. "I am indeed."

"Me too," I say, returning to my normal voice. "But Evie thinks it's perfect for us since I love puzzles and you presumably do too."

"Crazy for them," she says, emphasizing the words with passion. "My job is kind of like a puzzle. Being an ethical hacker. You have to get into everything backward." Then she talks more about some of the work she does, and it's fascinating. She practices hacking into security for banks, then giving them advice on where they have holes. "And it's sort of similar to what you do," she says. "Which is a puzzle too."

Instantly I know what she means.

"Since my patients can't talk?"

She smiles and nods. "Yes, that does make it quite a puzzle. It's like you need a whole other language."

We chat more as we weave through the moonlit streets in lower Manhattan, and as we do, I take a moment to admire her. I was being honest when I said if she wasn't pretty, it wouldn't matter.

And I meant it. To me, this kind of chemistry—instant and electric—matters so much more.

But I still find it kind of hard to believe she's as gorgeous as she is, and as interesting as she is. Clearly, something has to go wrong, like it did with Sandy.

I tense momentarily, picturing my ex.

Seeing her face.

Feeling the gut punch of her news that she was leaving on a jet plane.

But I don't want Sandy to infect this night.

I hoist those thoughts right out of my mind.

We stop at a light, and I put a hand on Olivia's arm then run my palm down her skin. "I hope I'm not being too forward by touching your arm."

She gazes at me. "You can definitely touch my arm. In fact, I hope I'm not being too forward by saying it gave me the shivers."

"Good shivers?" I ask as a cab screams by.

"Definitely the good kind."

"I can work with good shivers."

The light changes and we cross. "Good shivers are another item on the checklist," she says.

I mime checking it off.

She flashes a smile that ignites me, and I wonder why I took so long to say yes to Evie. But then the last time I felt this way was Sandy and—

Nope. Not going to do it. Not going to let her ruin the best night in ages.

No. *Years.*

Just focus on tonight.

When we arrive at the warehouse, the gamemaster opens the door and lets us inside, his tone that of a clandestine fellow from decades ago. "Hello, my secret agents. Welcome to the 1940s. We have your escape room ready for you."

The gamemaster ushers us down to a basement room, tells us our fellow agents were wrongly taken into police custody, and if we can find the clues and crack the case, we can set them free.

The clock is ticking.

I turn to Olivia. "Do you agree it would be completely embarrassing if we don't find our way out of here? After we both talked about our skill with puzzles?"

"Failure is not an option," she says, her tone intense.

Quickly and methodically, we survey the room. There are wigs, trench coats, mustaches, and maps of the world that look like they belong in an old-time professor's office. A framed portrait hangs behind a large oak desk with a green lamp.

The portrait features a stern-looking man. "His left eye is wonky," I say, pointing to the picture and the way the eye seems askew.

She peers more closely. "It sure is."

She spins around, counting quietly. "And there are nine mirrors in this room."

I catalogue the reflective surfaces—mirrors hanging on walls, one standing on a desk, another next to a globe.

"Mirrors and a wonky eye," I say, tapping my skull.

We spend the next thirty minutes with a laser focus, gathering clues, solving riddles, and cracking codes. We're nearly there. I can feel it. We stand at the desk, poring over one of the last clues, tossing ideas back and forth.

"This is so cool," she says. "If we're good at this, can we make it a thing?"

I laugh, loving that she's already decided we're having another date. "We can definitely make it a thing. We'll tackle all the escape rooms in New York City. How many do you think there are?"

"Thousands," she says softly, tilting her face toward me.

I hold her gaze, not wanting to look anywhere else but into her sparkling blue eyes.

"Olivia," I say, stepping closer to her, a rush of warmth skating over my skin, "are you telling me one hour into this date that you're having such a good time you want to go on a second date?" I don't know why I'm being so forward, yet I know exactly why I'm being so forward. Because she's fascinating. She's interesting. I've never felt this kind of instant, quick, sharp, spicy, tangible connection with some-body. Rather than run away from it, I don't want to let it go.

A lock of her hair is out of place, so I brush it off her shoulder. Her breath seems to hitch. "Yes. I do want to go on another date."

Somewhere in the back of my mind, I'm vaguely

aware of a ticking clock. But I want this more. I run the back of my fingers across her cheek. "Is kissing on your checklist?"

She gasps softly. "I would say kissing *you* is on my checklist, but you have to be a really good kisser to stay on my checklist."

I move my hand to her face, sliding my thumb along her jawline. "It's on mine too."

"Let's check it off." Her eyes flutter shut.

I lean closer to her and brush my lips over hers. I feel a whisper of breath that seems to ghost across her lips, and then the slightest gasp.

She trembles. I'm not even holding her or touching her, I'm just kissing her lightly, softly. And she's shuddering.

It's beautiful and too good to be true.

But it's all true, and it's happening.

She leans into me, inching closer. A soft sigh seems to fall from her lips, a sound that reveals how much she likes this soft, gentle kiss.

I want to know what else makes her feel this way.

I want to be the one to make her feel this way.

The intensity of those twin thoughts shocks me, maybe even scares me a bit, given my past experience.

But everything feels so right about tonight.

And I know that we could easily spend the whole night in here kissing, but I also suspect she'll be ticked if we don't get out of here before the clock.

I separate, even though my skin is buzzing, and my blood is humming. And I'd really like to do that again. Stat.

She blinks. "Wow, now my head is foggy. I don't know if I can concentrate."

"I don't know if I can either. But you know what I like more than kissing you?"

"I can't believe there's anything you like more than kissing me," she pouts.

I loop a hand around her hip, my thumb stroking against her. "I like getting to know you."

She practically purrs. "Herb, let's get the hell out of here, go to a diner, and get to know each other more."

We work, solving the final clue when we position all the mirrors in the room so that they're shining into the portrait's eye. As soon as they do, his eye works like a laser, then opens the door to the escape room.

We laugh and tumble out of the warehouse. The gamemaster tells us that was one of the fastest times that two people have actually executed an escape.

"Guess we had something we wanted outside of the room," I say, glancing at Olivia, who smiles back at me. We want to keep getting to know each other.

I thank the man and turn down the street, reaching for her hand.

She links her fingers through mine.

And am I ever glad I'm moving beyond the past.

Maybe this is insta-like. Heck, maybe it's insta-falling. But screw it. I'm feeling it everywhere.

We wind up at a nearby diner ordering burgers, French fries, and iced tea, and talking. We both agree Madison Square Park is our favorite park in the city, declaring the bench near the MetLife Building a great spot for kissing, then I tell her I like rock, and while she prefers pop, we agree we can coexist on the music front, since everything else is in sync.

Oh, and we also manage to squeeze in some diner kisses. She slides over to my side of the bench, and I wrap an arm around her shoulders, then bring her in close. As kisses go, this one is relatively chaste. We don't want to lose our diner privileges, after all. But the thoughts rushing through my head as I rope my hand in her hair and brush my lips to hers are anything but innocent. When I seal my mouth to Olivia's, I'm not only savoring this connection, I'm imagining where it'll lead to the next time, and the next. I'm picturing more nights, and dates that last well past midnight, and wind up in bed, tangled up together, sheets twisted, skin hot.

And the mornings too.

I'd like to wake up next to her.

I'd like to have breakfast with her.

I'd like to walk her home.

Holy hell, is this insta-something?

I've never been bitten by that bug before, but I'm feeling it now.

This woman and I—we just click.

And I don't want to play games.

We kiss and we chat until we close the place down.

At the end, it feels like we've been on three dates.

"Does this kind of feel like we've already hit the trifecta of three great dates?" I ask.

"It kind of does."

"And each one has been better than the last."

"They're all so good . . . it's almost as if it's too good to be true," she says, her tone light and breezy.

I stop, tug on her hand, and pull her flush against me. "But it's real." My voice is serious.

"It is?" Her tone is pocked with nerves. She looks unsure.

I nod, then cup her cheek and kiss her lips once more, savoring her taste, learning the flavor of her kiss, taking mental snapshots of how she feels in my arms.

Like she's giving herself to me.

And it's entirely what I want.

One freaking date, and I'm sold.

Yup, I've been bitten, and I don't want the antidote. I just want more.

"It's not too good to be true," I say as we break apart.

"Are you sure?" She seems even more flummoxed.

"I'm sure," I say, squeezing her hand. "Besides, who are we to argue with Evie?"

She laughs, but it sounds forced.

"Let me walk you home."

"Okay," she says, her pep and sass nowhere to be found.

That's okay. I'll provide the pep for two.

I take her hand, and along the way, I chat about the city, and the stores we pass.

"That coffee shop has the best vanilla lattes in the city. Don't tell anyone I drink vanilla lattes. But I'm just sharing that tidbit with you," I say, tipping my forehead to a trendy café.

"Oh. Okay."

I blink.

Her tone is . . . *off*.

That's odd.

But I keep going. "Best part of New York," I say, as a man scurries by, arms laden with delivery bags, a stuffed walrus poking out of the top of one, and a plastic robot popping its head from another, "is the delivery anytime anywhere of anything."

"Yes. Definitely."

There it is again.

She drops my hand.

Something shifts in her.

Her stance is stiffer. Her eyes are cooler. Her tone reads distant.

When we reach her place, I squeeze her hand. "You okay? You seem a little off now."

She gives me a huge smile. "I'm great, but I'm so tired, and I need to go. Bye."

She spins around, heads up her steps, and darts inside without a parting glance.

A kiss on the cheek.

Or another word.

I stand on the street wondering how we went from best date ever to what sure looks to turn into a ghosting.

And I've no clue what the hell went wrong.

5

Olivia

Misery is my companion.

It trips me up on the racquetball court the next morning.

With an unladylike grunt, I lunge for the ball, and I smack it wildly. It screams across the court, missing the mark by miles.

Flynn thrusts his arms in victory.

I'm not annoyed he won. I'm simply annoyed. With myself. My thoughts are only on Herb Smith, and how badly I botched last night.

"Rematch?" Flynn asks, eagerness in his eyes.

I don't have the energy to attempt to even the score with my brother. "Nah."

He sets down his racket on the bench. "Clearly something is horribly wrong. Confession time." He pats the wood. "Tell me how you messed up last night."

I can't pretend I didn't. Misery slithers down my spine. "We were having the world's most perfect date," I say, forlorn.

"Yeah, yeah, skip over the sex part."

"We didn't have sex."

"Okay, you didn't have sex, so how could it have been the world's most perfect date?"

I swat him with my towel. "Things do not have to include sex to be awesome."

"But sex does help to make things awesome."

"You know how you didn't want to talk about how I look good in clothes? I don't want to talk about sex with you."

"Okay, fine, so you're having an awesome date." He makes a rolling gesture for me to keep going.

"We hit it off, Flynn. We had insane chemistry. We talked about everything, including how much we liked each other already. That's what freaked me out. We liked each other from the beginning."

His brow knits. "So you're worried it's insta-love?"

"But I don't believe in insta-love."

"Except you felt insta-love for him?" he points out gently.

My stomach flips with the sweetest memories of Herb's kisses, his words, his easy way with me. "I did. That's the thing. I felt insta everything for him." I toss up my hands and look to my brother. "Clearly, there's no way that can work. It's impossible, so I took off at the end."

"That's real mature," he deadpans.

"I couldn't fathom that it was all real . . . And then, what if I'd invited him up?"

"Let's play this game," Flynn says, thoughtful and

logical. "What would have happened? What were you so scared of? Having real feelings for someone you truly like?"

A movie reel plays before my eyes. "I would have had hot, dirty sex with him, and I would have said, 'Let's get married and make babies,' and he'd have said yes, and it would be too good to be true."

"Wait. I thought we weren't supposed to talk about sex. You just said you had hot and dirty sex."

"In my dreams. Yes, it was going to be the hottest sex of my life because I'm that attracted to him. He kissed me in the middle of an escape room, and it was incredible. My toes are still tingling from it. Then he kissed me in the diner and all I saw was a future full of kisses and pancakes and conversations and hot, hot sex."

"This is like immersion therapy or something, right? Where you keep mentioning the deed over and over?"

I grab his arm for emphasis. "Yes, *the deed*. All the deeds. Over and over, but it was more than hot sex and dirty deeds. It was," I stop, remembering how easy everything was with Herb. Every. Single. Thing. "We connected. We hit it off. It was insta-love. And what the hell? That doesn't happen. And if it does, it's dangerous."

"Is it though? Is it dangerous? What if it's the real thing?"

My stomach flutters at the possibility. "It felt like the real thing."

"Why are you standing here with me, then?"

"I don't know. That's a good question." I swallow hard, my throat burning.

He sighs, shaking his head. "Olivia, you're doing it again."

I sigh. I don't fight the truth this time. "I know. I'm sabotaging it. Because I'm afraid."

"And you like this guy. So, woman up and un-sabo-tage it."

6

Herb

The morning brings no more answers.

Only a gigantic question mark when I check my phone and find zero messages from her.

Then again, I didn't text her either.

I don't need to have her reject me again. Doing it to my face last night was all I needed, thank you very much.

Still, the clinical part of me wants to understand what went down.

As the sun rises, I dribble a basketball on the court in Central Park then send it soaring into the net.

"And then she just left," I tell my buddy Malone, a fellow vet.

"Admittedly, that's not an ideal ending to a date." That's Malone for you. Straight up and to the point. He grabs the ball and whooshes it toward the net.

I snag it on the rebound. "It was literally the definition of a perfect date. Then she said, 'I'm so tired, and I need to go.' Boom. She was gone."

"Ah, now I get it. Sounds like she didn't want to see your sorry ass naked."

I roll my eyes. "My ass is spectacular, clothed or naked."

He shudders, like he's watching a horror flick. "Don't tell me anything more about your ass."

"I'm just saying, it's a gold-standard ass. She was checking it out."

He covers his ears. "Stop. Make it stop."

I shoot the ball, watching it arc into the net. "Anyway, that's that. She made it clear. There's nothing more that's going to happen. I'll just move on."

He grabs the ball, stops, and stares at me. "Wait. That's your takeaway?"

"Well, what should it be?"

"You like this woman, you had a great date, she turned sleepy at the end, and your conclusion is you should just *walk away*?"

"You said sleepy time isn't the ideal ending to a date."

He taps his chest. "I did, and it's not, because sexy time is the ideal ending to a date. But just because you didn't get *there* doesn't mean you stop shooting the basketball."

"I should throw a basketball to get to the sexy times?" I'm thoroughly perplexed.

"No. But here's the thing. You like her, you had chemistry, and you had one weird moment. Dating is weird. It's like when you put a sweater on a cat and they don't know how to walk."

I furrow my brow. "Pretty sure Olivia knows how to walk."

"But you might need to help her take off the sweater."

"Man, your analogy game needs work. Are you saying I need to undress her?"

"No. Well, not yet. But soon. What I am saying is you need to try again."

I crack up, clapping him on the back. "Wow. I didn't get that at all from the cat sweater analogy."

"Just try with her. Give it your best shot. Let her know what you want. The worst that'll happen is you're back out there on the dating circuit, putting sweaters on cats."

Maybe, just maybe, he's right. Maybe I should try to decipher what happened, because that really was the perfect date. And I don't want to give up this time.

7

Olivia

Later that day, I track down my matchmaker. We have lunch, and I tell her what happened.

"I really messed up."

Evie pats my hand. "No, sweetie, you didn't mess up, you got nervous. People get nervous. That's what happens. The question is—where do you go now?"

"I want to see him again. I think he's the one."

She beams. "I believe that too. But you're going to have to make it clear you're not a runner. That you're a stayer. Because I'm pretty sure he wants you to stay."

"Does he?" Tingles sweep through my body.

"The two of you are meant to be."

I quirk an eyebrow. "Do you believe in that? That people are meant to be together?"

"I do. Now you need to do what you should have done last night."

And I don't wait. I whip out my phone at lunch, dial his clinic, and ask to speak to Dr. Smith.

Evie beams the whole time, the proud matchmaker.

"He's with a patient right now. May I take a message?" The man on the other end of the phone asks.

With a smile, and a belly full of nerves, I give him a message. "Can you please tell Dr. Smith that it's Olivia and I would like to know if he would want to work on my checklist at Madison Square Park tonight?"

"I'll give him the message."

Evie claps.

I set down my phone, catching a glimpse of a message icon in the status bar. With butterflies fluttering, I click it open. It arrived fifteen minutes ago.

Herb: Hey, Olivia, so I'm not really sure what went wrong last night, but I'd like to try again with you. If you're up for it, maybe we can meet at Madison Square Park after work.

He must have sent it before I even called him. Oh God, I think I'm falling in love. My fingers speed through the fastest reply in the world.

Olivia: YES!!!!!! I'm there!

* * *

We arrive at the same time.

He walks toward me. I walk toward him. I stop in front of the bench, nerves and hope clogging my throat.

"I'm sorry I freaked out last night."

He sits and I sit next to him. "Are you a runner? Because once I have you as mine, I'm not going to want you to run away."

I take a deep breath. "I had a bad relationship. He cheated on me with a ton of other people, and sometimes I sabotage dates when it seems like it might work. I especially do when it's too good to be true."

He smiles and runs his thumb over my jawline. "So you think I'm too good to be true?"

"You said it yourself last night. Everything seemed that way."

"And that scared you?"

"It did. But that's no excuse." I reach for his hand. When he threads his fingers through mine, I swear all is right in the world. "Maybe it's too soon. Maybe it's too much. But I want to know what we can be."

He sighs, but it sounds like it's full of happy relief. "Look, I was hurt too. I was in love with this woman, and she took off around the world. I keep waiting for someone to pull the rug out from under me again."

My heart aches for him. "I don't want to pull the rug out from under you."

He sweeps his thumb over my jaw. "And I don't want to hurt you. All I want is to make you feel good."

And my heart—it soars to the sky. "That's the past. This is the present." I smile, and the way he smiles back at me, all crooked and sexy, sends heat through my body.

"There's only one way to find out if this thing is too good to be true," he says, his voice low, husky. His hand slinks around my neck, into my hair, sending shivers down my spine.

"To do this thing."

"Let's do this thing." He dips his face to my neck then

kisses me there. "You know what escape room I'd like to go to right now?"

"Which one?" I'm trembling with desire.

"There's one in my apartment."

I moan. "If you take me there, I'm not going to want to escape."

"That's the plan."

I plant a kiss on his lips, and it's better than last night. It's wonderful and magical, and I feel it everywhere. Everything else fades away but the absolute magic of this man and me. Maybe I'm crazy, but I swear I can taste forever in his kiss.

I make a choice.

To break my habits and make brand new ones.

Starting with the hot, dirty sex I'd hoped for.

Funny, how a man so sweet can be so dirty in the sack. Because when we make it to my apartment, the alpha animal in him comes out. And my sweet, swoony vet is whispering filthy things in my ear.

Things like . . .

Want to strip off all your clothes.

Spread you out on the bed.

Eat you, taste you, have you.

Fuck you.

Fuck you so damn hard you're not just seeing stars, but planets and galaxies.

Who knew that Herb Smith had such a dirty mouth?

"You are quite naughty," I say, shuddering as I grab his shirt, tugging it over his head as we stumble to my bed.

"I am. And hey, maybe that is what makes me too good to be true."

I laugh as I drag my nails down the grooves in his abs. *Grooves.* The man has traceable grooves. "Yes, definitely too good, because I do like it when you tell me all the bad things you want to do."

He yanks off my top, unclasps my bra, and dips his head to my breasts, murmuring as he licks a circle around my nipple. "I'd like to lick, and kiss, and fuck you all night long, Olivia. Take you hard, take you slow, take you every way."

I shiver. Is he for real? Is this happening?

My knees shake and I gasp as he lavishes attention on my breasts, telling me how delicious my skin is, how good I taste, how he could spend the night worshipping my body.

Yes.

I'd like that very much.

But I want to worship his too. And even when he has me squirming and panting, I don't let my own pleasure deter me. I sit up, pressing a hand to his chest.

"Let me taste you."

He arches a brow, his eyes darkening. "Yeah?"

"Let me show you how much I want you too."

"Show me," he says, more commanding than I expected.

He wraps my hair in a fist, and tugs me down to him. I'm hot and bothered and so ready for all sorts of dirty deeds as I take him in my mouth.

He moans and groans, muttering *just like that, yeah, deeper, your mouth feels so damn good, so fucking good*, that I swear I'm going to orgasm from his words. His reaction. His *realness*.

When his words turn into nonsense, he pulls me up, brings me close, and whispers *let me fuck you now, sweetheart.*

And yep. I'm done for. That's it. I'm gone. It's insta-lust, insta-love, insta-everything.

The deed is spectacular. It's electric and intense, it's wild and frenzied, it's slow and tender. It's the best it's ever been.

But it's not too good to be true. It's better.

I suppose that's how it goes when you've finally met the man who ticks all the boxes and then some.

* * *

Herb

The next morning I take her out for pancakes.

With her fork in hand, she dives in with gusto. "I love pancakes."

"Some people do."

"Hey! Don't rain on my pancake parade." She eyes my plate of eggs. "Why didn't you order pancakes?"

I sigh heavily and level with her. "I don't like them."

Her blue eyes pop. "What? How is that possible?"

"Just don't. I'm an eggs and hash browns kind of guy."

She shakes her head vehemently. "I refuse to believe anyone can dislike pancakes."

I tap my chest. "This guy does."

She huffs, takes another bite of her pancakes, then smiles. "Herb." She sets down her fork and gives me a strange smile.

"What? Is this a deal-breaker? A new act of sabotage?"

She stands, moves around the table, and sits down next to me, then kisses my cheek. "You told me you hate pancakes, and I still like you. This must be the real thing."

I laugh, cup her cheek, and bring her close for another kiss.

"And amazingly, I can tolerate the taste of pancakes on your lips."

She tap-dances her fingers down my shirt. "I'll get you to like them eventually."

"We'll see about that."

I walk her home, and outside her apartment she gives me the best redo ever—kissing the hell out of me and making me wish I could take the rest of the day off.

Instead, I peel myself away, send her a text, and ask if I can see her that night.

Seconds later, she replies with a yes.

It's possible I send her a few more texts that day. It's possible some are sweet. It's possible some are dirty too. She seems to like all those sides of me, and hell, I like all of hers.

Or really, *love* is the better word.

EPILOGUE

Olivia

I spend the night. And the next night, and the next one, and the next one.

For several wonderful blissful months that culminate in a ring, a promise, and a shared home.

Right now, I'm heading to meet Evie to thank her for setting me up with the man who has become my fiancé. When I see her at the coffee shop, Flynn is with her. "If we could only convince Flynn to let me work on him," Evie says, crossing her fingers.

He shakes his head. "Nope. I'm too focused on work."

I shoot him a *you're so ridiculous* look, then turn to Evie. "Someday he'll realize there is a meant-to-be for him, since I found mine. And we're going to Bora Bora for our honeymoon."

Flynn's green eyes light up. "He passed the Bora Bora litmus test."

"And someday you'll find someone who passes yours," I say.

My brother might be reluctant, he might have his own reasons for keeping up his guard, but I believe that deep down, there's a woman who's going to be his perfect match.

I found mine.

I thought he was too good to be true.

Then I realized that some things simply are, and those are the ones you don't let slip away.

THE END

Intrigued by Flynn? He has his own story to tell in COME AS YOU ARE, the smash hit romance that'll have you swooning, out now! Malone's story is told in SATISFACTION GUARANTEED, available everywhere!

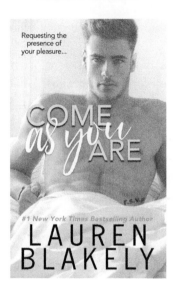

ALSO BY LAUREN BLAKELY

FULL PACKAGE, the #1 New York Times Bestselling romantic comedy!

BIG ROCK, the hit New York Times Bestselling standalone romantic comedy!

MISTER O, also a New York Times Bestselling standalone romantic comedy!

WELL HUNG, a New York Times Bestselling standalone romantic comedy!

JOY RIDE, a USA Today Bestselling standalone romantic comedy!

HARD WOOD, a USA Today Bestselling standalone romantic comedy!

THE SEXY ONE, a New York Times Bestselling standalone romance!

THE HOT ONE, a USA Today Bestselling bestselling standalone romance!

THE KNOCKED UP PLAN, a multi-week USA Today and Amazon Charts Bestselling standalone romance!

MOST VALUABLE PLAYBOY, a sexy multi-week USA Today Bestselling sports romance! And its companion sports romance, MOST LIKELY TO SCORE!

THE V CARD, a USA Today Bestselling sinfully sexy romantic

comedy!

WANDERLUST, a USA Today Bestselling contemporary romance!

COME AS YOU ARE, a Wall Street Journal and multi-week USA Today Bestselling contemporary romance!

PART-TIME LOVER, a multi-week USA Today Bestselling contemporary romance!

UNBREAK MY HEART, an emotional second chance USA Today Bestselling contemporary romance!

BEST LAID PLANS, a sexy friends-to-lovers USA Today Bestselling romance!

The Heartbreakers! The USA Today and WSJ Bestselling rock star series of standalone!

The New York Times and USA Today

Bestselling Seductive Nights series including

Night After Night, *After This Night*,

and *One More Night*

And the two standalone

romance novels in the Joy Delivered Duet, *Nights With Him* and Forbidden Nights, both New York Times and USA Today Bestsellers!

Sweet Sinful Nights, Sinful Desire, Sinful Longing and Sinful Love, the complete New York Times Bestselling high-heat romantic suspense series that spins off from Seductive Nights!

Playing With Her Heart, a

USA Today bestseller, and a sexy Seductive Nights spin-off standalone! (Davis and Jill's romance)

21 Stolen Kisses, the USA Today Bestselling forbidden new adult romance!

Caught Up In Us, a New York Times and USA Today Bestseller! (Kat and Bryan's romance!)

Pretending He's Mine, a Barnes & Noble and iBooks Bestseller! (Reeve & Sutton's romance)

My USA Today bestselling
No Regrets series that includes
The Thrill of It
(Meet Harley and Trey)
and its sequel
Every Second With You

My New York Times and USA Today
Bestselling Fighting Fire series that includes
Burn For Me
(Smith and Jamie's romance!)
Melt for Him
(Megan and Becker's romance!)
and *Consumed by You*
(Travis and Cara's romance!)

The Sapphire Affair series...
The Sapphire Affair
The Sapphire Heist

Out of Bounds

A New York Times Bestselling sexy sports romance

The Only One

A second chance love story!

Stud Finder

A sexy, flirty romance!

CONTACT

I love hearing from readers! You can find me on Twitter at LaurenBlakely3, Instagram at LaurenBlakelyBooks, Facebook at LaurenBlakelyBooks, or online at LaurenBlakely.com. You can also email me at laurenblakelybooks@gmail.com

Printed in Great Britain
by Amazon

36395698R10078